THE TEARS OF LOVE

Her father had died on their way home to England, his career in shambles, his name disgraced by accusations of treason. Now Cañuela Arlington and her mother were alone in London in desperate need of money. Cañuela would have to find work. Knowing her delicate beauty was sure to provoke unwelcome advances, Cañuela pulled her long golden hair back sharply from her face, obscured her dazzling grey-green eyes with huge glasses and dressed in unflattering black.

Her excellent qualifications soon interested an employer: Ramón de Lopez, the handsome Argentine aristocrat, one of the wealthiest men in South America. Cañuela trembled with rage at the mere mention of his name: Ramón was an "old friend" of her father's, one of the many who deserted in the crisis. Cañuela would repay him for his disloyalty. It would not be difficult to destroy him. If only he were not so wildly attractive . . .

BARBARA CARTLAND

Bantam Books by Barbara Cartland
Ask your bookseller for the books you have missed

1 THE DARING DECEPTION
2 NO DARKNESS FOR LOVE
3 THE LITTLE ADVENTURE
4 LESSONS IN LOVE
5 JOURNEY TO PARADISE
6 THE BORED BRIDEGROOM
7 THE PENNILESS PEER
8 THE DANGEROUS DANDY
9 THE RUTHLESS RAKE
10 THE WICKED MARQUIS
11 THE CASTLE OF FEAR
12 THE GLITTERING LIGHTS
13 A SWORD TO THE HEART
14 THE KARMA OF LOVE
15 THE MAGNIFICENT MARRIAGE
16 BEWITCHED
17 THE IMPETUOUS DUCHESS
18 THE FRIGHTENED BRIDE
19 THE SHADOW OF SIN
20 THE FLAME IS LOVE
21 THE TEARS OF LOVE

Barbara Cartland

The Tears of Love

THE TEARS OF LOVE
A Bantam Book / August 1975
2nd printing

Published simultaneously in the United States and Canada

PRINTED IN THE UNITED STATES OF AMERICA

AUTHOR'S NOTE

The descriptions of the British suspicions in 1892 that the United States was attempting to draw Argentina into the orbit of American influence by an offer of one hundred million dollars is accurate.

Secret reports in the Foreign Office show that both the French and the Uruguayan Ministries were agreed that the Americans had endeavoured to buy a Naval Base either in Argentina or Uruguay.

The golden age of Anglo-Argentine connections lasted from the Boer War in 1899 to the Great World Depression in 1928. During these years Britain was Argentina's best customer and Britain occupied first place as a supplier to the Argentine market.

THE TEARS OF LOVE

Cañuela, the daughter of a dead Diplomat accused in Argentina of being a traitor to Britain, hides with her mother in London under an assumed name. Because she has to earn her living she also hides her beautiful eyes behind close-fitting spectacles.

She obtains the post of secretary to Ramón de Lopez and he finds her knowledge of Spanish and Portuguese exactly what he requires. She hates him because he was one of the people who did not support her father at the time of his disgrace, but she is forced, through financial circumstances, to accompany him to Buenos Aires.

How Cañuela protects Ramón de Lopez from scandal, how she furthers his ambitions, how finally she saves him from the guerillas is told in this fascinating, dramatic, and passionate story set in Argentina just before the long successful years of Anglo-American co-operation in the frozen-meat trade.

ONE

1894

"It is no use, Mama! I cannot sew like you. I shall have to get some sort of employment."

The woman in the bed gave a little cry.

"No, Cañuela," she said, "I cannot have you going out to work! Besides, what could you do?"

Cañuela smiled.

"You forget, Mama, that I can speak Spanish, Portuguese, and a little Italian. I feel quite certain I could be a secretary to a business-man."

Her mother gave another cry of horror.

"It is impossible! What would your Papa have said?"

Cañuela crossed the room to sit down on a chair beside her mother's bed.

She put out her hand to lay it gently on the delicate white fingers on top of the sheet.

"Let us talk about this sensibly," she said in her soft voice.

"I am sure," her mother said, "I could do at least an hour's sewing a day."

"You must do what the Doctor told you to do," Cañuela replied, "and that is nothing!"

Mrs. Arlington gave a deep sigh.

"Is it really impossible to manage on what we have?" she asked in a low tone.

"I am afraid so," Cañuela said quietly.

"It is all my fault," Mrs. Arlington replied. "Those medicines are so expensive, and the extra food! Surely I do not need so many eggs, so much milk?"

She sighed again.

"I cannot bear to think of your working. There are men who will notice you and you are far too lovely, my dearest."

She spoke the truth, for Cañuela was indeed arrestingly beautiful.

Her features were almost perfect. She had a straight, aristocratic little nose and a heart-shaped face, but when people first saw her they noticed only her enormous grey-green eyes.

Her hair was a strange mixture of gold with touches of red, her lashes were long and dark, and her mother was well aware that wherever Cañuela went, men were attracted by her.

Ever since they had come back to England Mrs. Arlington's health had become progressively worse.

It stemmed not only from her desperate unhappiness over the loss of her husband, and the tragedy and adverse publicity which had surrounded his death. But also she and her daughter had been left with practically no money at all.

They had sold the few valuable possessions they had and for the last six months had been subsisting on what money Mrs. Arlington could earn by her exquisite embroidery.

There was a shop in Bond Street which would take as many of the embroidered satin and silk underclothes that she could make.

In fact the demand was far greater than she was able to supply.

While Cañuela could sew the seams, cut out the garments, and stitch on the lace, she could not embroider in the same delicate manner as her mother.

What was more, she took much longer over it and they were so behind with the orders that the shop was becoming disagreeable.

It seemed to Cañuela that the list of expensive foodstuffs and medicines that her mother required increased week by week.

At the same time Mrs. Arlington appeared to be getting weaker.

She was very thin, she coughed incessantly, and

there was a flush on her cheeks which looked unnatural against the whiteness of her skin.

"Do you think," Mrs. Arlington said hesitatingly after a moment, "that . . . people in . . . England will really require . . . secretaries who can . . . speak . . . Spanish?"

"There must be someone somewhere," Cañuela replied. "I saw in the newspaper the other day that this country is buying more meat from Argentina than ever before!"

She made an expressive gesture before she continued:

"That means that someone here is making contracts, someone is writing to the *Estancieros* in Argentina, and we know that few of them can speak English!"

Mrs. Arlington did not answer for a moment and then she said in a low voice:

"Your father had made such plans for you when you grew up. He always knew you would be beautiful and he saved so that we could give you a magnificent coming-out Ball, elegant gowns, and the chance to meet all the eligible bachelors available."

"Papa at least would have enjoyed the parties!" Cañuela said with a little smile.

"And you would have enjoyed them too," her mother answered. "What woman does not wish to be admired, fêted, flattered?"

Cañuela was silent. Then she said without any bitterness in her voice:

"It is no use crying over spilt milk, as my English Governess used to say."

"Poor Miss Johnson, I wonder what happened to her," Mrs. Arlington remarked. "But the person I often think about, Cañuela, is Maria. She was such a dear old woman and she loved us all so much."

"She worshipped Papa," Cañuela said. "I can remember now all the Italian lullabies she sang me when I was a baby, and she was still singing them when we went back to Buenos Aires."

She saw the distress on her mother's face and said quickly:

"We will not talk about it if you would rather not, Mama."

"I think about it all the time," Mrs. Arlington said, "of the last years when your Papa was doing so well, when everybody said that for his next post he would be given an Embassy in Europe . . . and then—"

She stopped suddenly and shut her eyes so that her daughter would not see the tears in them.

"Then it happened!" Cañuela said in a low voice, "and whatever anyone else may have said, you and I both know that Papa was innocent!"

"Of course he was innocent!" Mrs. Arlington exclaimed. "Do you really imagine he would ever have done such a thing?"

She drew a deep breath and her voice was strong as she said:

"He not only loved England, he also loved Argentina. He always said the country was in his blood and Buenos Aires meant home to him, as much as London."

"I remember Papa saying that," Cañuela agreed. "He used to say too that when he was away from Argentina he would dream of the Rio de la Plata, the campus and the people who were so warm and friendly towards him."

"Until the end!" Mrs. Arlington murmured.

Cañuela rose to her feet and walked across the room.

"I will never forgive the Argentines for the way in which they behaved," she said. "I hate them! Do you hear me, Mama? Hate them! Just as I hate those so-called friends of his in the British Legation who did not stand by him when things went wrong."

"They could not help themselves," Mrs. Arlington said. "Once a report had been sent to England your father had to come home to face an enquiry."

"And what did the Foreign Office expect to discover?" Cañuela asked.

"If only the map had not been missing," Mrs. Arlington said beneath her breath. "That is what was so damaging. On board ship your father would walk up and down the cabin night after night saying to me: 'Where could it be? What could have happened to it?' "

There was so much distress in her mother's voice

that Cañuela went back to the bed to take both her mother's hands in hers.

"Do not torture yourself, Mama. That is something we shall never know, and at least Papa died a hero."

Mrs. Arlington did not reply and both mother and daughter were thinking the same thing.

Lionel Arlington had dived overboard to save a little girl who had fallen into the sea.

He brought her safely to a boat which had been lowered from the ship to pick them up.

Then, inexplicably, when he should have been helped aboard, he vanished beneath the waves and was never seen again.

He was a strong swimmer and the sea was not particularly rough.

It was a mystery that having brought the child to safety he should then have lost his own life, unless—he had wished to do so.

The newspapers had made the very most of it. The headlines screamed:

DIPLOMAT UNDER SUSPICION DIES LIKE A HERO.
TRAITOR OR HERO?

There had been endless articles beginning:

Has there been a tragic mistake in suspecting one of our most brilliant Diplomats?

Through the kindness of the Captain of the ship which had brought Mrs. Arlington and Cañuela back to England, they had managed to evade the hoards of reporters waiting for them on the Quayside.

They had slipped ashore without being noticed. Then they had vanished.

The Press had tried to find them but without avail.

No-one suspected that the quiet Mrs. "Gray" who took a Bed-Sitting Room for herself and her daughter in a cheap Boarding-House in Bloomsbury was the much-sought-after widow of the dead Diplomat who had occupied the front pages of the newspapers for nearly a week.

No-one could have expected such an international

storm over an attempt by the United States of America early in 1892 to draw Argentina into the orbit of North American influence.

In March of that year, the British Minister in Buenos Aires had sent a report to the Marquis of Salisbury in England "in the strictest confidence."

It was rumoured, he said, that a Mr. Pitkin had made an offer to supply the Argentine Government with silver up to the sum of one hundred million dollars.

Before a reply could be received the British Minister went on leave and left Lionel Arlington, as *Chargé d'Affaires,* with this problem on his hands.

He became so worried about the American-Argentine negotiations that he sent off the longest ciphered telegram in the history of the British Legation.

But while in London Statesmen considered the situation in Argentina, where it was impossible to keep a secret, a seething controversy arose, all the more fierce and bitter because it was unofficial.

In London *The Times* published a brief account of American attempts to obtain a base on the River Plate.

This swept aside the secrecy and caused the American Minister to issue a public statement that the assertion was untrue.

The French Minister, however, was satisfied that these discussions had taken place, and both he and the Minister of Uruguay agreed that the Americans were endeavouring to buy a Naval Base either from Argentina or from Uruguay.

It was at this moment that a minor official, Janson Mandell, in the British Legation, supported by a dissident Argentine, sent a secret and confidential report to London.

Lionel Arlington, they alleged, was personally intriguing with the Americans.

It was totally and completely untrue.

The report was activated by jealousy and a personal vendetta, as the man in question had insulted Mrs. Arlington at a Ball with his attentions and had been knocked down and humiliated by her husband.

The accusations might have been ignored by the Foreign Office because the spectre, so alarming to the

British, of an American-Argentine alliance in fact soon disappeared, and the Americans embarked on a tariff-war.

This provoked the Argentine Government to lay an absolute prohibition on American petroleum, timber, and machinery.

Unfortunately Lionel Arlington's enemies, who should then have been forced to let the whole matter drop, discovered that a secret and very important plan of the harbour defences of Buenos Aires was missing from the British Legation.

It had last been seen in Arlington's hands, which he freely admitted.

But when asked to produce the map it had apparently vanished!

In the circumstances there was nothing the Marquis of Salisbury could do but recall Lionel Arlington to London for an enquiry into what had occurred.

No-one knew who gave the story to the Argentine newspapers, but it was not difficult to guess the informer's name.

Buenos Aires was at any time prepared to attack foreigners in their midst even though the money they invested in Argentina was of great importance to the country.

For a few weeks another "get rid of the foreigners" wave struck the city and resulted in a certain amount of rioting amongst the members of the Unión Civica Radical.

Arlington's name was bandied about as if he were a traitor rather than a man who had given many years of his life to Diplomatic relations between his own country and Argentina.

Sensitive, highly cultured, a man of great personality and integrity, he was shattered by the mere idea that anyone could imagine he could have behaved in such a manner.

As they sailed for home, sixteen-year-old Cañuela thought that her father had become an old man overnight.

Now, looking at her mother lying back against her pillows with so much of her beauty destroyed by suffering and illness, Cañuela told herself that not only had her father died at sea two years ago, but a part of her mother had died also.

"You are going to get well, Mama," she said suddenly. "We are not going to sit here in misery, hiding ourselves away and dying gradually of starvation. I am going to make money! Enough money at any rate for us to be comfortable."

"I cannot allow it, Cañuela," her mother replied. "You do not know what the world is like for someone as beautiful as you. You have always been chaperoned, as Spanish girls are chaperoned, and English ones too for that matter."

"You are talking about aristocratic ladies who can afford to do nothing," Cañuela answered. "We have no money, Mama, and therefore I have to make some!"

There was a sudden hard note in her voice that had not been there before.

As she spoke she walked across the room to a mirror which stood on top of a chest of drawers.

She looked at her reflection for a moment and then she undid her hair, which had been skillfully arranged in a chignon at the back of her head.

It tumbled over her shoulders, rippling like fiery gold almost to her waist.

Then she brushed it back from her oval forehead with a hard brush and, putting up her hands, twisted it into a rope which she pinned into a bun.

She pinned it so tightly with long hairpins that there was not a ripple in the smoothness of the hair which covered the top of her head.

She opened a drawer and, feeling at the back of it, drew out a pair of tinted, close-fitting spectacles that had belonged to her father.

He had worn them one Summer because he had hurt his eye in a riding accident and the Doctor had thought the light was too strong for the damaged retina.

She put the spectacles on her nose.

Because they had been fashioned for a man they were very large, and her small thin face seemed almost hidden behind them.

She turned round.

"Behold, Mama!" she said. "The efficient secretary!"

Mrs. Arlington stared at her daughter.

"You look terrible, Cañuela!" she said, "and those spectacles are positively disfiguring!"

"That is what I intend them to be," Cañuela replied. "You must admit, Mama, no man would look at me a second time."

"It is certainly a very effective disguise," Mrs. Arlington agreed.

Cañuela was wearing a black gown.

It was one of the very few she had. After the mourning for her father was over, she and her mother had not been able to afford to buy new clothes.

They had in their trunks the pretty gowns they had worn in Buenos Aires but neither of them could bear to think of the dresses, colours, and the luxury which belonged to the past.

Cañuela went to the wardrobe and took from the top shelf a small black bonnet.

It was trimmed only with black ribbons and even these she pressed down so that they would not look too smart or gay.

She tied it under her chin and covered the bodice of her dress with a tight black jacket which buttoned severely to the neck.

"I am going out," she said. "I shall be a little time, Mama, so do not worry about me."

"Where are you going?" Mrs. Arlington asked.

"To Brewstead's Agency in Piccadilly," Cañuela answered. "I remember when we were in London some year's ago I went with Papa there to engage an accountant for the Embassy in Spain."

"I remember that," Mrs. Arlington said in a low voice. "He was a very nice young man."

"I wish there was someone I could leave with you, Mama."

"I shall be all right until you come back," Mrs. Arlington answered. "But hurry, dearest. You know I do not like to think of you walking about the streets by yourself."

Cañuela gave a little laugh.

"I shall be safe enough looking like this," she answered. "The man who followed me from the shops yesterday would not give me a second glance today."

"A man followed you? Oh, darling, you did not tell me!"

"There was nothing he could do in broad daylight in a crowded street," Cañuela answered.

Mrs. Arlington's fingers trembled as she held them out towards her daughter.

"Do you really think you are doing the right thing?" she said. "If you were in an office with a man it would not be as safe as being in a crowded street."

"I promise you," Cañuela said soothingly, "I will choose my employer with great care. I will try and find someone as old as Methuselah and as rich as Croesus!"

Mrs. Arlington tried to smile but failed.

When Cañuela had gone she felt she should have protested more about her daughter's impetuous action in going in search of work.

She knew despairingly however that the little money they had would not last much longer.

She was well aware that Cañuela was getting thinner and was depriving herself of food so that she could buy the medicines that the Doctor kept prescribing despite the fact that they seemed, Mrs. Arlington thought, to do little good.

He was also expensive.

Because they were proud they insisted on paying him after every visit.

The future seemed so dark, so hopeless, that Mrs. Arlington lay back and shut her eyes.

First one tear and then another trickled down her cheeks.

"Oh, Lionel, Lionel," she whispered, "how can I go on without you?"

Cañuela reached Piccadilly after changing from one horse-drawn bus onto another. There were no incidents such as she usually encountered when she was out alone.

It had been impossible for her not to be aware that

her looks had an inflammable effect on men, and that while that often ensured her courtesy, assistance, and politeness, it also brought her a lot of unpleasantness.

Sometimes it was clerks and racing-touts who tried to get into conversation with her.

In the West End there were always top-hatted men who had the appearance of gentlemen but who did not behave like them.

Today for the first time she passed unnoticed and she thought with delight that her disguise was proving extremely effective.

She also hoped it made her look older.

Few employers were likely to believe that a girl of eighteen was as intelligent and proficient as she was at languages.

She had been born in Argentina, which accounted for her name, for her father and mother had been holidaying in the quiet, lovely village of Cañuela when she had arrived unexpectedly.

When she was five her father had been posted to Spain, and after three years in Madrid he had been offered a higher position in Lisbon.

From there they had returned to Argentina and for Cañuela, like her father, it had seemed like coming home.

Lionel Arlington had been like a boy showing her all the places he had known during his last appointment in Buenos Aires before he married.

They rode miles every morning into the fresh, green, empty land outside the city.

They set off on week-ends when the Legation was closed to explore the beautiful, lush, sunlit country which Cañuela grew to love as much as her father did.

"I am convinced," Lionel Arlington said once to his wife in Cañuela's hearing, "that this is the original Garden of Eden, and if I am Adam I could never ask for a more attractive Eve than you, my love."

Mrs. Arlington had laughed at him but there was an adoring expression in her eyes.

They were supremely happy together, which was fortunate because Mrs. Arlington, a daughter of Lord

Merwin, to the fury of her family had run away with an unknown, penniless young man in the Diplomatic Corps.

What had made her action worse was that at the time she was engaged to a nobleman of great importance, a fiancé chosen for her by her father.

"My family will never forgive me," Mrs. Arlington told her daughter, "not only because I married the man I loved but because I caused a scandal! In my father's eyes to appear in the newspapers, except when one is born or dies, was an unforgivable offence!"

Cañuela remembered those words when she realised that she could not buy her mother all the luxuries necessary for her health.

She had considered the idea of approaching her grandfather, if he was still alive, for help. Then she knew that not only would her mother forbid it, but he would undoubtedly refuse her request.

If he had resented the few paragraphs in the newspapers concerning the breaking off of his daughter's engagement, what would he think of the headlines, the editorial comments, and endless speculations about his son-in-law's supposed treachery and dramatic death?

"No. I have to look after Mama myself," she told herself, and reaching Brewstead's Agency she climbed the narrow stairs to the first floor.

Mr. Brewstead was an elderly, sharp-faced man with beady eyes who gave the impression that he expected every applicant who called to tell him lies.

He looked at those who sought employment with a disdainful air which made them feel humble and subservient from the moment they entered the Agency.

Any pretentions they might have about themselves quickly crumbled as he interrogated them skillfully from long experience and was able to extract information which they had been determined not to give.

For prospective employers he had an ingratiating manner which made them declare with satisfaction: "Brewstead is always so obliging!"

Cañuela waited her turn until a grey-haired man who was seeking a post as cashier had been humiliated into thinking he was in his dotage and long past being employed.

"I'll see what I can do," Mr. Brewstead said disparagingly, "but it's unlikely I'll be able to find you anything to equal the positions you have held in the past. You can call again tomorrow."

Dismissed with a look of something like despair in his eyes, the man turned away and Mr. Brewstead gave his attention to Cañuela.

His shrewd eyes observed the black dress. At once he was aware that the material was not of the best despite the fact that it fitted superbly.

He noted the plain bonnet, and his eyes lingered on Cañuela's glasses.

"Well?" he asked uncompromisingly.

"I am looking for a position as a secretary," Cañuela said.

"Anything wrong with your eyes?"

"Nothing, except I prefer to wear glasses."

Mr. Brewstead obviously tried to think of a retort for this but failed. He opened his ledger.

"Name?"

"Gray."

"Age?"

"Twenty-four."

Mr. Brewstead gave her a hard glance but made no comment.

"Address?"

Cañuela gave it slowly and it was written down.

"Qualifications?"

There was something in Mr. Brewstead's voice which told Cañuela that he did not expect her to have any.

"I speak Spanish, Portuguese, and Italian," Cañuela said, "and a little French."

She was pleased to see Mr. Brewstead look surprised as he wrote this down without comment.

"Can you use a typewriter?"

"Yes," Cañuela replied, "and I can also use a shorthand of my own which is quick enough to follow most people's dictation."

She thought as she spoke how lucky it was that her father had always used her as his unofficial secretary when he was at home.

"We do not want the staff of the Embassy coming here at all hours," he used to say. "Cañuela can do all I want done. I like my home to myself."

Sometimes when he had reports to submit he would tell the Legation that he would not be in for two or three days, and they would play truant, riding away from the city on one of their explorations.

Cañuela would take down his reports in the evening after they had spent the day in the saddle, and would spend half the night typing them out for him.

It had all been great fun and she had loved every moment of it.

Now she was glad that it gave her qualifications that even Mr. Brewstead found impressive.

"Let me see your references," he said in a tone of one who likes to find fault.

"I am afraid I have always worked abroad," Cañuela replied. "It therefore will take a little time to write to my previous employers and ask them to speak on my behalf."

Mr. Brewstead put down his pen.

"Surely," he exclaimed, "you had the common sense to ask for written references before you left your last employment?"

"As a matter of fact, I did not think it necessary," Cañuela replied in a lofty tone. "I did not expect to have to work when I arrived in England, and therefore at the time a reference did not seem necessary."

She paused to add:

"However, if one is required I will be able to produce it, but not of course at a moment's notice."

Her explanation sounded plausible even to herself and Mr. Brewstead stared down at what he had written.

At that moment a man came into the Agency.

He was middle-aged and dressed neatly if inconspicuously.

He walked up to the desk with an air of authority and Cañuela stood aside for him.

"Good-day, Mr. Hayward!" Mr. Brewstead said effusively. "We were not expecting to see you back so soon!"

"I am afraid," Mr. Hayward replied, "the young man you sent us was hopeless—quite hopeless. His Spanish was slow and laboured and his Portuguese nonexistent!"

"Tut, tut. I am indeed sorry," Mr. Brewstead apologised. "His references were excellent!"

The middle-aged man gave a faint smile.

"The standard of Spanish which the English find adequate is useless where my employer is concerned."

"I can only apologise," Mr. Brewstead said, "and hope that we can find you someone else. But quite frankly, Mr. Hayward, we have no young man on our books at the moment who can speak anything but his native tongue."

Mr. Hayward sighed.

"I know it is difficult," he said. "You have done your best, but unfortunately it does not solve my particular problem."

He turned as if to leave the office and Cañuela, who had stood to one side, listening to everything he said, moved forward a step.

"I can speak Spanish and Portuguese."

Mr. Hayward turned to look at her.

"Really!" Mr. Brewstead ejaculated. "The gentleman would not consider employing a female."

"Why should that matter if he cannot find a man to fill the position?" Cañuela asked.

Mr. Hayward was looking at her. Then he said:

"Are you really proficient in Spanish?"

"I can speak it as well as I can speak English," Cañuela answered.

"And Portuguese?"

"I lived in that country for five years."

Mr. Hayward hesitated and then he said to Mr. Brewstead:

"It may be hopeless to make such a suggestion, but perhaps Mr. Lopez would consider this young woman."

"Then why not take her with you?" Mr. Brewstead suggested. "The answer can only be 'no.'"

"That is true," Mr. Hayward said. "Will you come with me, Miss . . . ?"

"Gray," Cañuela answered.

"I have a carriage outside," Mr. Hayward said. "If you are not suitable it can bring you back within half an hour."

"Thank you."

"I can only hope, Miss Gray," Mr. Brewstead interposed sharply, "that you have told us the truth and that you speak these languages as well as you say you can. Mr. Lopez is very particular."

"Very particular indeed!" Mr. Hayward confirmed with a sigh. "Do not let us waste any more time, since Mr. Lopez was extremely annoyed at finding that the young man you sent was so ignorant. It has been a difficult morning, I assure you!"

"I'm sorry—I really am!" Mr. Brewstead said. "Let us hope Miss Gray will be able to fill the gap."

There was something in his tone which told Cañuela he thought it very unlikely.

He was however clutching at straws to save his own face.

Without saying any more Mr. Hayward led the way down the stairs and meekly Cañuela followed behind him.

As she went she was wondering who Mr. Lopez might be.

It was quite a common name both in Spain and in Argentina.

There were aristocrats and beggars called Lopez in both countries.

Whoever this Lopez might be, he obviously impressed both Mr. Hayward and Mr. Brewstead.

There was a carriage waiting in the road outside.

A footman opened the door and with an effort Mr. Hayward remembered his manners and let Cañuela step in first.

He followed her to sit beside her on the back seat, holding his hat in his hand and twisting it agitatedly.

"You are quite sure, young lady, that you can speak fluent Spanish?" he asked as the carriage started off.

"I promise you that I am bilingual," Cañuela said reassuringly.

"My employer is difficult—very difficult!" Mr. Hayward said. "He wants perfection. He expects people to be as quick as he is himself, and he is intolerant—very intolerant indeed—of people who make mistakes."

Cañuela thought he sounded abominable, but she said pleasantly:

"Is your employer Spanish?"

"No, indeed. He is an Argentine," Mr. Hayward replied.

Cañuela stiffened.

"He is Señor Ramón Mendoza de Lopez!" Mr. Hayward went on.

Cañuela drew in her breath.

Now she knew of whom they had been talking: Ramón Mendoza de Lopez was one of the most talked about and admired men in the whole of Argentina.

He was a representative figure of the powerful élite who had emerged as the result of the rapid expansion of the economy.

Vaguely she remembered, although she had never seen him, that he was spoken of as being handsome, and he was famous for his feats of gallantry and gambling. As a youth he had run through one fortune and made another.

He was an aristocrat in that his direct ancestors were Spanish and had come to South America as conquerors.

She thought that his mother had been English but it may have been his grandmother.

She had been interested in him because her father had spoken of him so often.

She remembered that he had helped to found the Jockey Club, and her father had said that he was immensely rich and one of the most able of the wealthy land-owners, having an understanding of the financial and political possibilities of the country.

"One day Ramón de Lopez will be President of Argentina," Lionel Arlington had said once.

"Why do you think that?" Cañuela asked.

"The people want someone to worship," her father said with a smile, "and Ramón de Lopez fulfills all their romantic dreams of what an Argentine should be."

He was speaking half-cynically, and yet Cañuela thought that he admired and perhaps envied the rather flamboyant young man who had so much wealth and everything else to his credit.

And yet, she told herself, Ramón de Lopez was, she was sure, one of the men who had hounded her father when the map of the harbour was missing.

There had been a number of them who had spoken against him, given newspaper interviews, and urged the British Legation that Lionel Arlington should be sent home.

She was almost certain that Ramón de Lopez was amongst them, but if she did not remember, her mother would.

As a surge of hatred swept over her at what the Argentines, even those who had pretended to be friends, had done to her father, she wanted to stop the carriage and get out.

Then she told herself that perhaps it was fate that he should come into her life at this particular moment.

Perhaps she would have a chance to avenge her father; to destroy an Argentine as he had been destroyed by them.

"I hate them! I hate them!" she wanted to shout aloud, and realised that she was tense as the carriage drew up outside an imposing house in a street off St. James's.

"This house belongs to the Argentine Government," Mr. Hayward explained, "and Señor Lopez stays here when he is in London. He has a private apartment on the first floor. The offices are on the ground level and the upper floors."

Once inside the house he led the way past a number of liveried footmen.

There was an impressive Waiting-Room in the front part of the house, into which he showed Cañuela.

"If you wait here, Miss Gray," he said, "I will find out if Señor Lopez is in and if he will see you."

He paused and added:

"You do understand, he may not consider even for a moment the employment of a woman?"

"I realise I am privileged to have come as far as I have, considering the unfortunate accident of my birth!" Cañuela replied with irony.

Mr. Hayward looked at her with what she thought was an expression of dismay and then he went away.

Cañuela laughed. Then she realised that that sort of remark would quickly ensure her return to Brewstead's Employment Agency.

"I must be humble," she told herself, and felt something strong and resolute inside herself rebel against the thought.

"You should be proud," her father had said to her once, "proud of yourself so that you can hold your head high and look any man in the face! It is only cowards and boot-lickers who crawl about waiting for people to kick them."

'Father was kicked when he least expected it,' Cañuela thought bitterly.

She wished she could remember if Ramón de Lopez had really been one of the men who had snarled at him in his hour of need.

'If only I could do to them what they did to Papa!' Cañuela thought vindictively.

She remembered how her proud and sensitive father had suffered when they had left Buenos Aires, and there had only been two or three people to see them off.

How unlike other times when they had gone on holiday with a cabin packed with presents of flowers, fruit, chocolates, and books.

Then there had been dozens of friends to bid them *Bon Voyage* and to urge them, "Hurry back—we cannot do without you."

How different it had been when they had crept out with the vile accusations hanging over them like a cloud, her mother in tears, her father white-faced and grim.

"I hate them! I hate the Argentines! I will never go back there!" Cañuela vowed.

The door opened.

Mr. Hayward stood there.

"Señor Lopez will see you, Miss Gray."

Cañuela rose.

For a moment she did not wish to meet Señor Lopez. Something, although she was not quite certain what it was, seemed to warn her against going upstairs. Something told her to run away.

Then she knew that she was being nonsensical.

She was here in search of a job, and who was more likely to employ her than an Argentine who required a secretary who could speak fluent Spanish and Portuguese?

At the same time, as she followed Mr. Hayward up the stairs, she told herself that the job, whatever it was, was not likely to last long.

Ramón de Lopez was likely to be in England only for a short visit.

If she was clever she could perhaps earn enough money to last for a month or so after he had gone.

At any rate she was determined that her mother should have all the small luxuries the Doctor had prescribed for her as essential.

Mr. Hayward stopped at a door on the first floor.

He turned the handle quietly.

"Miss Gray, Señor," he said respectfully, and Cañuela walked forward.

It was a large, luxuriously decorated Sitting-Room with sofas and chairs in front of a marble fireplace. The long windows looked out over St. James's Park. A huge crystal chandelier hung from the ceiling.

It was all very impressive, but no more impressive than the man who rose from the flat-topped desk which stood at one end of the room.

Cañuela had expected Ramón de Lopez to be handsome, after what her father had told her, but she had not thought that he would be so tall, so broad-shouldered and at the same time so elegant.

He had a lean face with clear-cut features, a square chin, and dark, deep-set eyes beneath straight eyebrows. His black hair was brushed back to show a well-shaped head.

There was something autocratic about Ramón de Lopez which was, Cañuela thought, apparent the moment you looked at him.

He was an aristocrat; a man born to command; a man who gave orders and expected them to be obeyed, and would be surprised if they were not!

There was also, she thought, a ruthlessness about his mouth and something that made her feel suddenly shy in the scrutiny in his eyes.

He stared at her as if he was searching for something, as if he looked not only at the superficial appearance of a person, but deep into the soul.

Then she told herself quickly that she was being imaginative.

She was endowing Ramón de Lopez with the glamour he commanded in Argentina and had nothing to do with the work she would have to do for him.

"Sit down, Miss Gray."

Ramón de Lopez indicated with his hand a chair in front of the desk.

Cañuela sat herself on the edge of it.

She did not know why, but she felt nervous.

There was something overpowering about him, she thought, something which made her feel that he pierced her disguise and knew that she was hiding her identity from him.

"I understand from Mr. Hayward that you are proficient in Spanish. Is that so?"

"Yes," Cañuela replied.

Without altering the tone of his voice he began to speak at a tremendous speed, concerning his work in England for the Argentine Meat Trade.

He spoke of negotiations and discussions that were taking place which he hoped would lead to advantageous contracts.

He finished what he was saying with a question.

Without pausing, Cañuela answered him in Spanish.

Knowing it was expected of her, she spoke at some length.

When she had finished there was just a faint hint of surprise in his eyes.

Then without a pause he continued to converse, but this time in Portuguese.

Again Cañuela replied as soon as he had finished.

She knew that her Portuguese was even purer from a linguistic point of view than her Spanish and she wondered if Mr. de Lopez would notice.

He did!

"You speak excellent Spanish, Miss Gray," he said in English, "and I am surprised that many of the words I used and which you repeated in reply to me, you pronounced with an Argentine accent."

Cañuela did not answer.

She wished now that she had stuck to the more formal Castilian Spanish which she had spoken in Madrid.

"How can you speak so well?" Ramón de Lopez asked.

"I have studied both languages," Cañuela replied.

She spoke in a cool, repressive tone which she hoped made it quite obvious that she did not wish to answer questions.

"Can you use a typewriter?"

"Yes."

"And shorthand?"

"I can take dictation at a normal speed."

"Would you call the way I have just been speaking 'normal'?"

"More or less. I might find some of the business terminology a little difficult at first, but I would soon get used to it."

Ramón de Lopez toyed with an ivory paper-knife which had lain on the desk beside him.

"I think you have realised, Miss Gray, that I wished to engage a man?"

Cañuela inclined her head.

"But I understand from Mr. Hayward that there is no-one available at the moment, and as I am pressed for work and with a great number of cables to be decoded every day, I must have an assistant now."

He paused as if he expected Cañuela to speak, and when she did not do so he said:

"How soon can you come to work for me?"

"Tomorrow," Cañuela replied.

Ramón de Lopez rose to his feet.

"Very well then, Miss Gray. I would like to start you on a weekly basis as I am not yet sure how long I shall be staying in London. But I will be frank with you and say that if I find a male secretary in the meantime, I would feel free to dispense with your services."

"I quite understand. A woman must always take second place," Cañuela said.

She regretted her words as soon as she had spoken them and wished that she had said nothing.

She saw the sharp glance Ramón de Lopez gave her and felt sure that he was not used to having secretaries who were anything but complete and absolute door-mats.

"Very well, Miss Gray," he said, "I shall expect you to be ready to start work at nine o'clock tomorrow morning."

"There is one other thing, Señor Lopez," Cañuela said. "I would like to know what salary you are offering for the post."

"Of course," Ramón de Lopez said with a twist of his lips. "That is, of course, a matter of the utmost importance. What are you asking?"

The question took Cañuela by surprise. For a moment she could not think of a reply and then she said:

"I am afraid I have no idea what is the correct salary in England. Up to now I have worked abroad."

"As I have no idea either," Ramón de Lopez said, "we shall have to enquire."

He hit a bell on his desk with his hand and it rang out sharply.

The door opened and Mr. Hayward came in so quickly that Cañuela was sure he must have been listening outside the door.

"Hayward," Mr. de Lopez said, "what salary was I intending to pay the young man who was not worth sixpence?"

Mr. Hayward named a sum which made Cañuela draw in her breath.

It was more—much more than she had anticipated a secretary to be worth!

"Very well," Ramón de Lopez said. "I hope, Miss Gray, that meets with your approval."

"I am prepared to accept," Cañuela said, "provided if I start work at nine o'clock I may leave at five."

Ramón de Lopez raised his eye-brows.

"I might expect you to stay longer," he said. "Cables

have an inconsiderate habit of arriving late in the afternoon."

There was silence.

Then he said with what Cañuela thought was a note of amusement in his voice:

"What you are really saying, Miss Gray, is that if I keep you late you will expect to be paid overtime? I am sure Mr. Hayward will see that you are justly and adequately recompensed."

"Thank you," Cañuela said.

She dropped a small curtsy.

With something like consternation she realised that it was something she should have done upon first entering the room.

She turned and walked towards the door, hoping that she appeared composed and that Ramón de Lopez had no idea how quickly her heart was beating.

TWO

"Here is the report, Señor."

Ramón de Lopez looked up from the desk at which he was writing and Cañuela thought that there was an expression of surprise in his eyes.

"The report I gave you yesterday?"

"Yes, Señor."

He took it from her and she knew from his attitude that he was sure because it had been done so quickly it must be full of mistakes.

His next words confirmed this.

"Sit down, Miss Gray. There may be a number of alterations required and I might as well explain them to you as I read it."

Cañuela sat down on the chair she had occupied when Señor Lopez had engaged her three days earlier.

She thought as he sat back and opened the papers she had typed for him that she hated him more every time she came into his presence.

She had not been mistaken in thinking that he was one of the men who had deserted her father when he had most needed a friend.

"Señor de Lopez?" her mother had said slowly when she had returned home to say that she had found employment.

Then with a little cry Mrs. Arlington had added:

"No! Not Ramón de Lopez!"

"Tell me what you remember about him, Mama."

"Your father was so fond of him. He admired him and the way he was trying to institute reforms in the country. . . ."

Mrs. Arlington paused.

"When Papa was accused of treachery, he was one of those who intrigued against him," Cañuela interposed.

"Not positively," her mother replied, "but he never came to see your father, not even when he wrote to him."

"Papa wrote him a letter?" Cañuela asked.

"Yes," Mrs. Arlington replied. "He was feeling so desperate, so depressed, so absolutely appalled at the lies that were being spread about him that he wrote to Señor Lopez, asking his advice."

Mrs. Arlington's voice was hard as she went on:

"The man whom your father had considered to be a great friend for so many years did not even deign to reply."

"It is hard to believe!" Cañuela exclaimed. "Was the letter sent by hand?"

She knew that the post in Buenos Aires was often erratic.

"Your father sent it by one of our most trusted servants," Mrs. Arlington answered. "If the Señor had not been at his house in the Plaza St. Martin, it would have been sent immediately by one of his numerous staff to his *Estancia* which is less than two hours' ride from the city."

"I remember it! Of course I remember it now!" Cañuela cried. "I never went there, but Papa once pointed it out when we were riding in that direction. He said it was one of the most magnificent and up-to-date *Estancias* in the whole country."

"The Señor is a very wealthy and very influential man," Mrs. Arlington remarked.

She accentuated the last adjective and Cañuela said:

"I loathe him for what he has done to Papa, but I will work for him because he pays well, and I shall hope that in some way or another I can avenge Papa."

"No! Do not speak like that," Mrs. Arlington begged. "It is unlike you, Cañuela. You know as well as I do that hatred is dangerous, not only for the person against whom you direct it, but for one's self."

A little smile came to Cañuela's lips.

"That is what you taught me when I was very young, Mama, and in consequence I have tried all my life never to hate anyone. But you cannot expect me to feel anything but loathing for those who were responsible for Papa's death."

The words seemed to create a stillness in the room.

It was the first time that either Mrs. Arlington or Cañuela had ever voiced aloud the thought which was always in their minds—that Lionel Arlington's death had not been an accident.

"Surely you could work for someone else?" Mrs. Arlington said after some time.

"I doubt if anyone else would pay as well," Cañuela replied, "and anyway, it will not be for long, Mama."

Perhaps, she thought to herself, Ramón de Lopez would sack her as he had threatened to do at the end of the week if she was not satisfactory, or if he found a man to replace her.

In the meantime her mother could have milk and cream, eggs and grapes, and the young, tender chickens which the Doctor had insisted she needed.

'And while I take his money,' Cañuela thought, 'I can hate him and hope that in some way it will hurt him!'

The high wages that Señor Lopez offered were some consolation for her feelings.

After she had left him, Cañuela had taken a horse-drawn bus towards Bloomsbury, then changed to another which dropped her near the shops where she made her daily purchases for their food.

She had been worried as she journeyed home because of leaving her mother for so many hours alone.

Mrs. Arlington could in fact move about the room by herself but it was the thought of her loneliness which perturbed Cañuela.

It seemed to be a part of her mother's illness that she grew more depressed and more miserable every day.

At first she had wept bitterly whenever she thought of her husband, and that was more understandable and in a way more natural than a limp apathy.

Now she seemed to wake more despondent every morning and find it a tremendous effort to take an interest in anything.

Cañuela would chat away, trying to bring a smile to

her mother's face, but it was inevitable that most of their conversations would be of the past.

At times she thought despairingly that the light had gone from her mother's eyes and nothing she could do or say would ever kindle it again.

She alighted from the bus into the crowded street and made her way to the small grocery shop where the owner, a bald, genial old man, showed all his customers courtesy and consideration.

"Good afternoon, Miss Gray," he said when Cañuela appeared. "What can I do for you today, and how is your poor mother?"

"My mother is very much the same, thank you, Mr. Robinson," Cañuela replied, "and I have quite a list of things I require, if you would be kind enough to allow me to bring you the money at the end of the week?"

"Of course, Miss Gray."

Cañuela ordered more than her usual number of purchases and then she asked:

"I was wondering, Mr. Robinson, if you happen to know the address of that nice little lady who was in here the other afternoon and who you told me was a retired school-teacher?"

Mr. Robinson was an inveterate gossip. No sooner had someone left his shop than he was always prepared to draw a thumb-nail sketch of their history, their character, and their interests.

"You mean Miss Graham," he said. "A very nice lady, but I fear she has fallen on hard times."

"That is what you said before, Mr. Robinson," Cañuela confirmed. "I would like to get in touch with her if it is possible."

"You have perhaps heard of something that might be to her advantage?" Mr. Robinson asked with undisguised curiosity.

"Something like that," Cañuela replied evasively. "Where does she live?"

"Only round the corner, as it happens," Mr. Robinson answered, "in a small room hardly big enough to swing a cat, so my son says, who delivers her groceries from time to time. But then, as I expect you know, Miss, it's difficult for people in that position to save."

"I am sure it is," Cañuela agreed, "and the address?"

"Twenty-two Museum Lane," Mr. Robinson replied. "Now, Miss, allow me to send young Joe along with your purchases. He'll be there within half an hour."

"That would be very kind as long as he will not be any longer," Cañuela answered. "I must cook my mother something nourishing for her supper."

"He'll be with you almost before you get home, Miss," Mr. Robinson promised.

Cañuela left the shop and went to 22 Museum Lane.

Miss Graham was at home.

A woman of over sixty, she looked thin and pale, which Cañuela guessed came from not eating enough.

She smiled at Cañuela with pleasure when she opened the door.

"May I speak to you for a moment, Miss Graham?" Cañuela enquired.

"Of course, Miss Gray. Do come in. I am afraid my room is very small, but to me it is home."

It was spotlessly clean and tidy but, as Mr. Robinson had said, extremely small.

The bed which stood in one corner had been converted to a sofa for the day-time and decorated with a few painstakingly embroidered cushions.

One wall was entirely covered with books, and a cupboard concealed not only clothes but all the implements necessary for cooking on the gas-ring which stood in the fireplace.

There was just room for a very small arm-chair and an upright one besides a table which could be folded and placed in front of the window.

Cañuela sat down in the arm-chair and her hostess took the other.

"I came to see if you could help me, Miss Graham," she said.

"How can I do that?" Miss Graham replied. "I will do my best if it is within my power."

As she spoke there was a look in her eye which was half of fear, half of wariness.

Cañuela realised almost in horror that Miss Graham thought she might have come to borrow money from her.

"I have just found employment," she said quickly. "It is an excellent post although it may not last long, and I am worried about my mother."

There was an expression of relief on Miss Graham's face which told Cañuela that her suspicion had been right.

"I do not like leaving my mother alone from early morning until late in the evening," Cañuela explained, "and I wonder, Miss Graham, if it would be possible for you to come and spend some time with her, at least for a few hours a day?"

"Of course, Miss Gray," the elderly school-teacher replied. "It would be a pleasure!"

"I would of course wish to remunerate you," Cañuela said.

"It would be an honour and a pleasure to be with your mother," Miss Graham repeated firmly, "without there being any question of payment."

"You must understand we cannot impose on your good nature," Cañuela said with a smile.

As she saw that Miss Graham was going to insist on refusing, she said quickly:

"You are proud, but so are we; and besides, Miss Graham, I would like to share my good fortune in getting such lucrative employment. As I say, it may not last long."

"Then you must save for your mother from what you make," Miss Graham said.

"Shall we put it this way?" Cañuela suggested. "I will pay all your expenses and that would include travelling from here to where we are living."

She smiled.

"Shoe leather is just as pricey as taking a bus-ticket and I would also be very grateful if you would do some shopping for me. If I am kept late by my employer, the shops might be closed and I would not wish my mother to go hungry."

"That would be unthinkable, Miss Gray."

"If you would cook her luncheon—it is most important she should eat at regular times, the Doctor has said—and share it with her, then I should be more than grateful."

"I do not like to take your food, Miss Gray," Miss Graham protested.

"But I know Mama would not wish to eat alone," Cañuela replied.

Finally Miss Graham accepted what seemed a ridiculously small sum for the services she was willing to give. At the same time Cañuela was aware that it would help her.

It would also be of inestimable benefit for her to be able to have a meal that she did not have to pay for.

Cañuela was quite certain that there would also be innumerable cups of tea or coffee that the two older women could enjoy together.

Mrs. Arlington accepted the arrangement without protest.

Cañuela had the feeling that she found it an effort to argue about anything, least of all about plans which concerned herself.

She was far more worried about Cañuela.

"Are there a lot of men in the house where you will be working?"

"A great number of them," Cañuela answered, "judging by what I saw when I went up and down the stairs. But do not worry about me, Mama. They looked at my spectacles and never gave me another glance!"

"I am not surprised!" Mrs. Arlington exclaimed.

For the first time she smiled.

"Take them off, Cañuela, I cannot bear to see you looking like that. Your Papa always detested ugly women!"

The next day when she was shown her office, which opened off the large, luxurious Sitting-Room where Señor Lopez worked, Cañuela found that there was a great deal for her to do.

She was astonished at the number of ciphered cables that he sent and quite horrified at the expense of them.

Ciphered cables of some length would cost one hundred pounds or more and it was obvious to Cañuela that her employer did not for a moment study the cost.

Cables shuttled backwards and forwards between England and Argentina like flights of birds.

It was clear to Cañuela at once that Señor Lopez was engaged in very complicated negotiations in respect of not one commodity but half a dozen.

Argentina was not only concerned with the export of frozen meat, a trade which was increasing year by year, but was also selling wool in large quantities, and the exports of cereals, wheat, and linseed were increasing year by year.

It was not surprising, Cañuela thought, that the landed class and the controllers of the supporting commercial structures were growing enormously rich.

Buenos Aires was becoming a synonym for wealth and luxury.

Before she left Argentina she and her mother had laughed at the Magnates who hired private railway-trains to transport their establishment from their Winter residences to their Summer homes.

One *Estanciero* even took his own herd of milking cows to Europe to ensure that his children had the right milk to drink.

What was more, the Jockey Club in the Calle Florida was a centre not only of recreation for the élite like Señor Lopez, it was also a treasure-house of books and works of art which her father had often described to her.

Cañuela knew that wealth in Buenos Aires was most unequally distributed.

Yet few Argentines were as desperately poor as the people she had seen in the back-streets of London.

In Argentina food was abundant, cheap, and good.

Her father had always said that the reason that the men and women in the country were predominantly big, healthy, and good-looking was the fact that their immediate forebears knew little of the malnutrition, cold, and persistent ill-health that was to be found in the slums of England.

But the aristocracy of Argentina had everything, Cañuela thought now, and looking at Señor Lopez as he read the report she had typed for him, she felt that there was an arrogance in his air of ease.

It was one of the things she resented about him, she

thought, and why hidden behind her tinted spectacles her eyes blazed hatred as she looked at him across the desk.

He was so supremely self-confident, so sure of himself. There was too a look of the buccaneer about him, as if he was determined to take by force anything he could not gain any other way.

His clothes were well-tailored and obviously from Saville Row.

They were English and fitted him without exaggeration, and yet she thought he wore them with an air which made him seem raffish, even if one could not actually find any fault in his appearance.

Perhaps it was his almost exaggerated good looks, besides a personality that Cañuela knew would be outstanding even in a roomful of other men.

He turned page after page of the report without comment.

She knew with a feeling of satisfaction that there was an expression of astonishment on his face when finally he put the report down on his desk and said:

"This is very good, Miss Gray. I was expecting it to be but the first draft of many, but it can go just as it is."

Cañuela rose to her feet.

He did not hand her the report as she expected; instead he said:

"Where can you have learnt to write such a complicated report so well?"

Cañuela did not answer and he said:

"I asked you a question, Miss Gray."

"In my last employment," Cañuela replied.

"And where was that?"

"Abroad."

"In what country did you work last?"

"Portugal."

"Can you in Portugal have had so much experience of the business terms of Argentina?"

Again Cañuela did not answer and Ramón de Lopez said:

"Again I ask you a question, Miss Gray."

"You have finished with the report, Señor," Cañuela said. "If I take it now it will catch the next post."

Ramón de Lopez sat back in his chair.

"In other words you do not intend to answer my questions?"

"No!"

"You think I have no right to ask?"

"They are irrelevant to the work I am doing here."

"On the contrary, I think them very pertinent."

There was a pause and then he said:

"I can see, Miss Gray, that I was rather remiss at our first interview. An employer should ask such questions of an applicant. I imagined that such preliminaries had been carried out by Mr. Hayward, but he informs me that you have told him nothing about yourself."

"No!"

"Why not?"

"He did not ask me."

"And you do not think I am entitled to ask questions now?"

"I hoped, Señor, I was giving satisfaction."

"You know you are, Miss Gray. I have never, and I can say this in all sincerity, known anyone who could make out a report such as you have done at the first attempt, so competently or as quickly."

Cañuela inclined her head as if she accepted the compliment with restraint.

Again there was a pause and then Ramón de Lopez said:

"I am curious about you, Miss Gray. It is unusual to find, shall I say, someone of your breeding working for her living."

There seemed no comment that Cañuela could safely make to this, so she merely waited.

"You live at home?" Ramón de Lopez asked.

"I live with my mother."

"And she is content to allow you to come out to work?"

"Yes."

The word seemed to be dragged from between Cañuela's lips and Ramón de Lopez gave a little laugh.

"You are longing to tell me it is none of my business," he said. "I know that even though I cannot say I see it in your eyes! Do you have to wear those spectacles? I should have thought they made your work more difficult."

"I have to wear them," Cañuela replied.

"You look like a little owl in them," he said, "but of course a very wise owl. We have quite a number of them in Argentina and there is a small grey and white one with a pretty dove-like voice which hoots round one's house in the evening."

Cañuela drew in her breath.

She knew the owl he spoke of so well.

How often had she listened to its musical voice when she and her father and mother had been out in the country?

For a moment the thought of it gave her an almost unbearable feeling of home-sickness for the days when she had been so happy and everything had seemed filled with sunshine.

There had been wide open spaces. Even to think of them conjured up the scent of wild thyme, of flowering beans and lucerne.

But she said nothing and after a moment, with the sound of what could be interpreted as one of exasperation, Ramón Lopez held out the report towards her.

"Send it immediately, Miss Gray," he said, "and then come back with your note-book. I have another longer and even more complicated one to give you."

Because Cañuela knew that her reserve and silence irritated him, it seemed to her that in the next few days he deliberately challenged her.

He would talk at an incredible speed and it was only because she understood the subject on which he was speaking that she managed to get it down in the shorthand she had invented for herself.

Sometimes he would get up from his desk and walk across the room and dictate while looking out over the green trees in St. James's Park with his back towards her, so that it was hard to hear what he said.

Because she knew that in some unspoken way he was fighting her, she fought back.

She would not admit defeat, and although sometimes

she invented what she did not hear, she did it so skillfully that he was not aware of it when he read the reports.

More than once he tried to trip her into revealing the actual places where and people for whom she had worked.

By training herself to answer his questions in monosyllables and say nothing when the question was too difficult, Cañuela knew with satisfaction that she was winning the secret battle between them.

If she had not been so consumed by her hatred, she told herself, it would have been impossible not to admire the manner in which Ramón de Lopez was winning concessions and fantastic contracts for Argentina.

He was negotiating not only for his own produce but for a dozen other *Estancieros,* or cattle-breeders, all of them owning thousands of acres of the lush pastureland which was making Argentina so wealthy.

It was fantastic to remember that the first sheep had been introduced into Argentina in only 1550, and two years later seven cows and one bull were the foundation of the mighty herds now scattered all over the Campo.

It was the Spanish Colonialists who recognised the suitability of the Pampas for stock-breeding. But it was many years before the cattle-owners had the idea of exporting anything beyond hides which they sold to Spain and Brazil.

Cañuela could remember her father telling her how in 1882 an Argentine business-man had converted his merchant ship, called a *saladero,* which supplied the domestic market with dried and salted meat, into a *frigorifico.*

From that moment it was possible to convey frozen meat to Europe and England.

Lionel Arlington had laughed as he told the story.

"In England, the land of conservative tastes, frozen mutton did not flow instantly into the kitchens."

"Why not?" Cañuela asked.

"A London wholesale dealer called Tallerman encountered serious opposition from the butchers of Manchester when he tried to break into the market."

"What did they do?"

"They offered to handle Argentine frozen mutton at threepence a pound!" he replied, "which of course was only a way of saying no."

"What happened?"

"Tallerman decided to circumvent the butchers by setting up a stall of his own in Knot Hill Market."

Lionel Arlington smiled.

"Tallerman said that at first he had no customers, but he cheered up when he saw one or two women buying a pound or half a pound of meat and returning shortly, accompanied by their friends who also came to buy."

"And the word went round?" Cañuela cried.

"It did!" her father answered. "The year that Tallerman beat the butchers of Manchester, over seventeen thousand frozen carcasses were exported from Argentina to Britain. Six years later the trade grew to nine hundred thousand carcasses."

"It must have been very satisfactory!" Cañuela exclaimed.

She knew now that the total was increasing fantastically year by year.

Ramón de Lopez's contracts would make Argentina richer than it had ever been before.

She found the work she was doing fascinating.

It was not only because of the figures and calculations which had always interested her. It was because as she worked she could visualise the great herds spreading out over the land under the warm golden sunshine.

With them would be the *gauchos* riding as if they were part of their horses, puffing away at their cigars and wearing their huge silver spurs with the same kind of arrogance which characterised Ramón de Lopez.

One satisfactory thing was that Cañuela could answer her mother's questions in the evening quite truthfully and say that no-one had paid her any unwelcome attention.

Because she worked exclusively for Señor Lopez the other clerks in the building treated her with respect and kept their distance.

The gentlemen, the traders and other men who

visited Ramón de Lopez in large numbers every day, never gave her a second glance.

It was a relief at night to take off her close-fitting spectacles, to undo her hair and let it fall over her shoulders in great waves as if it was glad to be free of the tight confines of the bun into which it was constrained every morning.

One evening she looked in the mirror before she went to bed and wondered without meaning to do so whether Ramón de Lopez would think her attractive if he saw her without her disguise.

Among the duties with which he had entrusted her after she had been with him a day or so was not only the ordering of the bouquets of flowers which he sent to women in great profusion but also the purchase of presents for them.

He would tell Cañuela to buy several huge bottles of French perfume or a dozen long kid gloves or a satin hand-bag.

These she ordered from shops in Bond Street where he invariably had an account.

There was a parasol with the handle set with jewels for one lady-friend. For another a pair of opera-glasses made of gold and tortoise-shell.

He apparently trusted her judgment, for one afternoon he called her into his room, and lying on the desk in front of him she saw a number of glittering diamond bracelets, each in a long velvet box.

"I want your advice, Miss Gray," Ramón de Lopez said. "I am choosing a rather special present and I do not want to make a mistake. As a woman, which do you think the most attractive?"

Cañuela looked at the bracelets and realised that they must have cost an astronomical amount of money.

Several in her opinion were in good taste but the others were flashy.

She looked at them for a moment before she said:

"It very much depends, Señor, for whom the bracelet is intended."

He glanced at her sharply.

"What do you mean by that?"

"Exactly what I say," Cañuela replied coldly. "For

an actress or someone who would wish to attract attention, it is quite obvious that those on your right are the most suitable. For a lady, those on your left."

"You are very perceptive, Miss Gray," Ramón de Lopez said, "and are you curious to see which I shall choose?"

"It does not concern me, Señor," Cañuela answered.

Without waiting or asking his permission to withdraw she walked from the room, closing the door behind her.

She felt that in some way he deliberately tried to needle her, and it made her hate him all the more furiously.

And yet she found it impossible not to think about him; not to be acutely conscious of him even when she was working in the next room.

"I hope this job does not last long," she told herself.

Yet when the end of the week came she could not help being overwhelmed by the enormous sum of money she had earned.

Ramón de Lopez had in fact kept her late on three occasions.

The extra payments gratifyingly swelled her salary, but for a moment she contemplated telling him that she would not accept them.

When she had asked if she might leave at five o'clock she had not been thinking of anything except leaving her mother by herself.

Because he assumed that she was being difficult for mercenary reasons she thought now that she would take the money and say nothing about it.

What did it matter if he thought she was grasping?

She had earned every penny he gave her because she was more proficient in her job than anyone else he was likely to find in England.

Who else would not have to have explained and certainly spelt for them words peculiar to Argentina that were used in the letters to the *Estancieros* and the Board of Trade in Buenos Aires?

Who else would find it easy to understand some of the phrases and words that were not pure Spanish but were new words that had not only been adopted from the *gauchos* but also varied immigrants who had come to the country after the Spanish conquerers had left?

Poles, Turks, French, Russian Jews, and Germans. They had all contributed their individual imprint to the language.

"He is very fortunate to have me!" Cañuela told herelf.

Nevertheless she felt slightly guilty as she went home to her mother with more money than she had thought it possible for any woman to earn in so short a time.

There was no doubt that Ramón de Lopez was a success in London.

Every day invitations from all the most important hostesses were placed on Cañuela's desk for her to open, sort, and ask for his instructions.

"Do you wish to dine with the Prime Minister on Wednesday?" she would ask.

"I suppose I shall have to go."

"And there is a Foreign Office Reception the following night."

"I can hardly get out of that."

Amongst the social invitations there were a number of letters which were essentially personal.

Cañuela opened one of these by mistake and had read the first sentences before she realised, the colour rising in her face, what it contained.

It was certainly not intended for her eyes!

She had unfortunately slit open the letter with a paperknife and there was nothing she could do but replace it in its envelope and put it on Ramón de Lopez's desk.

After that she was extremely careful not to open any letter which looked as if it came from a woman.

Some were scented, which made it easy, but she grew adept in recognising a feminine hand and these she placed unopened on his blotter and presumed that he attended to them.

Sometimes notes arrived with a smartly uniformed groom waiting outside for an answer.

Ramón de Lopez also began to give her orders to reserve tables for dinner or supper at Restaurants; purchase his theatre-tickets, and make sure that the carriages conveyed his guests when he was otherwise engaged or too lazy to collect them himself.

It was not difficult for Cañuela to learn that he took an interest in Sylvia Standish, a dancer who was appearing at the Gaiety Theatre.

Night after night she would have to instruct a carriage to wait for her at the stage-door when the show was over.

In a burlesque called *Don Juan,* which Cañuela thought was an appropriate title, Sylvia Standish was the star. She was a fairy-like creature who charmed everyone with her grace, piquancy, and poetry of motion.

There was also a French actress called René Lefleur, who obviously attracted Señor Lopez.

Once she called at the office.

She had a fascinating face with a wide gamin mouth and a voice which made everything she said sound seductive.

Her clothes were chosen to attract attention, her diamonds were blinding.

Cañuela could hear Ramón de Lopez and René Lefleur laughing unrestrainedly in the next room. She wondered what they found so amusing, and the actress's exotic perfume lingered on the air long after she had left.

A table was permanently reserved for Ramón de Lopez at Romano's in the Strand.

It was a gay supper-place where her father used to tease her mother he had once taken a leading-lady.

He then found that she had ordered such an expensive meal he had the greatest difficulty in paying the bill!

There were other night-clubs, supper-Restaurants which Ramón de Lopez obviously found amusing but which Cañuela was quite certain no lady would visit.

She could quite imagine that most London actresses would find him alluringly attractive.

He was very different from the *effete* aristocrats who usually waited at stage-doors and gave expensive parties where they would drink champagne out of a satin slipper.

Sometimes Cañuela would wonder if she would have enjoyed the London Balls to which this year she would have been invited when her father came on leave.

She would have been presented at Court, wearing three white Prince of Wales's feathers in her hair and with a train falling from her shoulders over her white gown.

She would have been presented together with the rest of the Diplomatic Corps, who were always the first to make their curtsies to the Queen in the Ball-Room at Buckingham Palace.

There would have been dinner-parties at which she would have met girls of her own age, all discreetly chaperoned by their fathers and mothers.

She would have been able to dance with the eligible bachelors who every night would throng the Ball-Rooms of the great mansions in Park Lane, at which the Prince and Princess of Wales were the most sought-after guests of honour.

Despite every resolution, Cañuela could not help a little sigh.

How different everything would have been if the United States had not thought it a good idea to have a Naval Base in Argentina!

Then she told herself sharply that day-dreams would get her no-where.

"I have to look after Mama. I have to make her well. Perhaps one day she will be able to meet her friends again."

It was worse, Cañuela thought, for her mother than it was for herself because Mrs. Arlington had always enjoyed the social world.

She had been a charming and efficient hostess.

Looking back, Cañuela could hardly remember a day when somebody had not been entertained in their house whether they were living in Madrid, Lisbon, or Buenos Aires.

She was quite sure that most of their English friends would not have believed the libellous accusations that had been printed about her father and would have been only too willing to show kindness and hospitality to his widow.

But Cañuela knew that her mother would never put herself in the position of being embarrassed or snubbed by those who had once predicted that her father would be one of the youngest and most brilliant Ambassadors in Europe.

"The higher they rise the further they fall!" she told herself bitterly.

She knew it would give her a great deal of pleasure to watch Ramón de Lopez fall!

She had been working for three weeks and she fancied that Mrs. Arlington was looking better.

Miss Graham had been a great success. She was an intelligent woman and Mrs. Arlington liked having her to talk to. The two women appeared to have much in common.

It was a relief for Cañuela too. She was often very tired by the time she had struggled on and off buses, or if when they were full she had walked half the way home, and it was nice to find that Miss Graham had made everything neat and tidy.

Usually too there was a meal left for Cañuela so that she did not have to cook anything for herself.

Her mother's bed had been remade and she would be lying back against her pillows, waiting to listen to what Cañuela had done during the day.

Cañuela soon realised that her mother steeled herself to hearing news of Argentina—in fact she wanted to talk about it.

Where she worked there were Argentine newspapers and magazines to read or borrow, so there was always some item of gossip about past friends for her to bring home.

Babies were born, people got married, and Mrs. Arlington seemed more and more to enjoy hearing about the life in which she had once played an important part.

Then one evening, just as Cañuela was getting ready to leave, she heard Ramón de Lopez's bell.

She walked into his room. He was standing with his back to the mantelpiece.

She advanced a little way and stood waiting for him to speak to her. As she did so she noticed that he had a cable in his hand.

She realised it was not one that had been brought up to her, which she would then have passed on to him.

She thought vaguely that it must have arrived as he came into the house and he had therefore picked it up in the Hall.

It seemed to her that there was an unexpected silence, then almost as if he was choosing his words Ramón de Lopez said:

"I have to leave for Buenos Aires at the end of the week!"

Cañuela had always been expecting that he would tell her this sooner or later, but now that the moment had come she felt a momentary regret.

It was hard to think that she would no longer be earning the large salary he had paid her and that she would have to go back to Brewstead's Agency to find another job.

"You do not express any sorrow at my imminent departure?" Ramón de Lopez remarked with a touch of sarcasm in his voice.

Cañuela realised it must have seemed rude that she had said nothing.

She had been thinking only of herself.

"I apologise," she said quietly, "but I was quite aware that you would have to leave sometime."

"I want you to come with me!"

For a moment she thought that she had not heard him aright, and then she said quickly:

"It is impossible!"

"Why is it impossible?" he enquired. "I have a great number of reports that I must write on the voyage, and you know as well as I do there is no-one who can do them except yourself."

"I am sorry, but I cannot come with you."

"Why not?" he asked.

Cañuela did not reply and he said:

"I imagine, since you tell me you are living with your mother, that you support her by your earnings. That will be taken care of, she shall not suffer by your absence."

"I would not contemplate it!" Cañuela said firmly.

"If I take responsibility for your mother," Ramón

de Lopez insisted, "surely you can spare the time to come with me, if only as far as Buenos Aires?"

"No!"

"Damnit all!" he said with a sudden note of irritation in his voice, "why must you be so difficult? Any other woman of your age would jump at the opportunity to go abroad, see the world, to travel in luxury."

"There can be no question of my accompanying you, Señor," Cañuela replied.

Without waiting for him to say more she went from the room.

She had a sudden urgency to be free of the place—to be at home. She felt almost as if he were reaching out towards her with tentacles like an octopus from which she could never escape.

She knew only too well how determined he could be if he wanted something which he found difficult to get.

He was right when he said that there was no-one, at any rate in his office, who could possibly do what she could do for him on the voyage.

But the idea of accompanying him was unthinkable.

First, she could not leave her mother. Second, how could she ever go back to Buenos Aires?

Because she was somehow afraid of Ramón de Lopez's persistence, Cañuela felt that she could not return to the office the next day.

She would write to Mr. Hayward and ask him to send her the money she was owed, or perhaps she would even forfeit it.

Then she knew she needed that money; needed it for her mother and therefore she must go back.

It would be only for a few days and however much he might argue with her, or even try to cajole her, there was nothing he could do if she continued to say no.

"He will miss me," she told herself. "I am glad about that."

She wondered too if he would miss the ladies in whose company he had spent so much of his time while he had been in England.

She thought of all the presents she had bought for them.

Sometimes they had been for Society ladies and the recipient's beautiful aristocratic face was to be seen in the fashionable magazines.

Having tried not to be interested, having told herself it was none of her business, Cañuela nevertheless found it hard not to look at the pictures or to remember the names.

It was raining when she stepped down from the crowded bus to walk the last part of the journey home.

Incredibly she felt depressed when she reached the poor street in which they lived and saw the shabby front door of the Boarding-House, which needed painting.

She walked into the small Hall which seemed always to smell of cabbage and climbed the narrow stairs to the first floor, where their room was situated.

She had her hand on the handle of the door when it opened and to her surprise she saw the Doctor.

"Good evening, Dr. Lawson," she exclaimed.

"Miss Gray, I hoped you would return before I left. I want to speak to you."

Cañuela thought he would go back into the room. Instead he came out onto the landing and shut the door behind him.

"I was sent for because your mother was taken ill."

Cañuela gave a little gasp.

"What has happened?"

"She is all right at this moment," Dr. Lawson replied. "My first visit was early this morning."

"Why did you not let me know?" Cañuela asked. "My mother knows where I am working."

"I made her comfortable," Dr. Lawson said, "and this afternoon I came back with a Specialist."

Cañuela pulled off her spectacles. Her eyes were on the Doctor's face and she was very pale.

"What is wrong with my mother?" she asked, and the question was almost beneath her breath.

"I will speak frankly," Dr. Lawson answered. "Your mother has tuberculosis. I suspected it and the Specialist has confirmed my diagnosis."

Cañuela gave a little gasp and he said gently:

"It is not very bad and there is every hope that she

can be cured if it is possible for her to have the proper treatment."

"Where?" Cañuela asked, and her voice was hardly above a whisper.

"The Specialist says that she must go to Switzerland immediately," Dr. Lawson replied. "There is a Clinic in the mountains which he confidently recommends. Once she is there, he thinks in perhaps three months the patch on your mother's lung would heal."

Cañuela drew in a deep breath.

"How much would that . . . cost?"

She could hardly bring herself to say the words.

She knew only too well that however little it might be it was beyond their resources at the moment.

"I had already anticipated that question," Dr. Lawson said gravely. "I have therefore considered it, and the very least you would need, including the journey and medical expenses, would be two hundred pounds!"

THREE

"May I speak to you, Señor?"

Ramón de Lopez looked up from the newspaper he was reading to find Cañuela standing at his side.

He had not heard her come in.

As he looked at her he realised that she was nervous.

"But of course, Miss Gray," he replied. "What can I do for you?"

"You asked me yesterday, Señor," Cañuela replied, "if I would come to . . . Buenos Aires with . . . you."

"And you refused me very positively."

"I . . . I have . . . changed my mind. I will come if you still . . . want me."

"Of course I want you. I made that very clear."

There was a pause and then Cañuela said in a low voice:

"But if I . . . come, I shall require a sum of . . . two hundred pounds to be paid before I . . . leave England."

Even as she spoke it seemed to her an enormous amount of money to ask, and despite her resolution to remain cool and calm she felt the colour rising in her cheeks.

She was also angry with herself because her fingers were trembling.

"Two hundred pounds?" Ramón de Lopez said slowly. "I think I can understand, Miss Gray, that someone has used a little more intelligence in this matter than you did."

"What do you mean?" Cañuela asked before she could stop herself.

"I am guessing," Ramón de Lopez replied, "that your young man realised your worth and knew that such a nest-egg would be a sensible beginning of your saving for the future."

Cañuela raised her chin.

"It is nothing like that!" she said sharply.

"Your young man did not suggest it?"

"I have no young man."

"You really expect me to believe that?"

"You can believe what you wish, Señor," she said. "The truth is . . ."

She stopped suddenly realising that she was about to tell him something about herself—a thing she had not done since she had first entered his employment.

"I am waiting," Ramón de Lopez said quietly.

Cañuela did not speak and he said:

"I would like to know the truth."

"It can be of no interest to you," Cañuela protested. "I am prepared to come with you to do the work you require. Unfortunately I cannot arrange it unless I can first have that particular sum of . . . money."

She spoke firmly, but at the same time she could not prevent herself from gripping her fingers together.

It was difficult to lower her pride and beg for money.

And yet, she told herself, what did it matter as long as her mother could get well?

Ramón de Lopez's eyes were on her face.

After a moment he said:

"I am perfectly prepared to give you any reasonable sum which you think essential, Miss Gray. At the same time, as your employer, I wish to know why it is so important to you."

For a moment Cañuela thought of defying him.

She had the feeling that he was enjoying her discomfort.

Then she told herself that it was not of the least importance what he thought or what he felt.

All that mattered was that her mother should get to Switzerland.

At the same time it went against the grain to give in to him.

He was fighting her, she thought, simply on a matter

of principle because he could not tolerate being opposed by a woman and not having everyone who worked for him a complete door-mat beneath his feet.

"I am still waiting, Miss Gray," he said after a moment, and she fancied that he was well aware of the conflict within her.

"My mother has to have special . . . treatment," she said.

It sounded as if the words were being dragged from her.

"Where?"

"In Switzerland."

"I am sorry that she is ill."

"Thank you."

"I will instruct Mr. Hayward," Ramón de Lopez said, "to write you out a cheque immediately for two hundred pounds. I will also tell him to add to it another hundred pounds for your expenses in coming to South America with me."

"As you will be paying my fare, I imagine I shall have no expenses," Cañuela said sharply.

"I suspect you will find there will be quite a number of unavoidable extras," Ramón de Lopez contradicted. "You will need new clothes, for one thing. The climate is not the same as here."

"I am aware of that," Cañuela said.

"Since you have been working for me," Ramón de Lopez went on as if she had not spoken, "your wardrobe has not been very varied . . . I am therefore prepared to pay for the clothes that you will need both on the voyage and when we arrive."

"You do not imagine, Señor, that I would allow you to pay for my clothes?" Cañuela said proudly.

"Do not be so nonsensical!" he replied. "You know as well as I do that you cannot afford the expense, if your mother is ill, of buying a number of things you would not have thought of purchasing had you not been in my employment."

It was true, but to Cañuela there was something degrading in feeling that she must accept anything so intimate from him as the clothes she wore on her body.

Then she remembered how much a hundred pounds

more would mean to her mother, and even while she thought of the sum she had an idea.

She drew a deep breath.

"I will accept the extra money, Señor. It is of course the same as a . . . lackey's livery being paid for by his . . . employer."

She saw a sudden glint in his eye as he replied:

"Exactly the same, Miss Gray! But a lackey would doubtless feel beholden to be a little more civil!"

Cañuela realised even as he spoke that she had struck him and he had struck back.

The honours were even!

"I can quite see," Ramón de Lopez said with a sarcastic note in his voice, "that we shall have a very pleasant trip, Miss Gray!"

"I shall be there to do your work, Señor," Cañuela replied.

She hated him the more because he was smiling.

Nevertheless when she took the cheque home that night she could not help feeling excited because she could now make immediate plans for her mother to go to Switzerland.

"I have another idea, Mama," she said. "You shall take Miss Graham with you."

Her mother looked at her in surprise and Cañuela went on:

"You know it would really be impossible for you to travel alone. In fact I am sure Dr. Lawson assumed that I would accompany you. But you can take Miss Graham and it will be a wonderful holiday for her. You can keep her out there with you quite a long time."

"But you will want the money yourself for your clothes," her mother replied.

Cañuela laughed.

"Do you really think I am going to spend money like that on clothes when I have all I need in the trunks that have never been unpacked since we came back to England?"

"I had forgotten about them!" Mrs. Arlington exclaimed.

"But I had not!" Cañuela said. "Some of the gowns I

wore two years ago would now be too childish, but yours would fit me perfectly, and you know as well as I do, Mama, you are much too thin to wear them now."

Unable to wait to find out if her idea was feasible, Cañuela dragged the trunks into the room from where they had stood outside in the passage ever since they arrived.

They were made of best leather hide, and although the gowns inside were creased they had come to no harm.

Cañuela shook out the gowns and tried on some of them.

"They really do fit you!" Mrs. Arlington exclaimed.

It was true.

There was very little to be done to them, and what was necessary Cañuela could do at night and Miss Graham in the day-time.

Even her mother insisted on sewing on new ruffles, fresh collars, and mending a torn flounce.

There was a profusion of pretty muslin gowns that Mrs. Arlington had worn when it was hot. They were in gay colours and all of them in the most exquisite taste.

"They are too good for me," Cañuela said as she laid them out on her mother's bed.

"Your Papa always wanted me to look smarter than any other Diplomat's wife!" Mrs. Arlington said with a smile. "I am afraid, because he encouraged me, I was often very extravagant!"

"You were also right up to date with the fashion, which has altered very little in the last two years," Cañuela said.

This was true. The bodices were still very tightly moulded over the figure, the skirts were full, draped, frilled, or flounced, and the evening-gowns were décolleté and off the shoulders.

"I shall not need any evening-gowns," Cañuela said.

"You must take them with you," Mrs. Arlington replied. "You never know; Señor Lopez may wish you to go with him to a Reception or even invite you to a dinner-party. I would not have him ashamed of your appearance!"

Cañuela laughed.

"I should look ridiculous in one of those glorious evening-gowns with my owl-eyes."

Her mother looked surprised and she explained:

"Señor Lopez asked me if I must always wear my spectacles. He said I looked like an owl!"

"I want to tell you to take them off," Mrs. Arlington said, "but I am afraid of what might happen if you did."

"So am I," Cañuela agreed. "Not that it would make any difference where Señor Lopez is concerned. He hates me just as I hate him!"

"He hates you?" Mrs. Arlington exclaimed.

"We are having a 'Battle Royal,' Mama," Cañuela laughed. "He tries to get the better of me and I am determined to be as irritating as possible!"

"Then why is he taking you with him?" Mrs. Arlington asked.

"Because he cannot find anyone efficient to take my place," Cañuela replied with satisfaction. "I am certain if there was anyone else who could do his work he would drop me like a hot brick. As it is, because I am useful he has to make the best of a bad job!"

"I do not like to think of your working in such circumstances," her mother said slowly. "At the same time it is better than when I could not sleep or bear to let you out of my sight for fear of what might happen."

"Papa's spectacles have been a God-send," Cañuela said. "And now, Mama, I had better hang up these gowns so that some of the creases will fall out before they are ironed."

"Miss Graham will do that for you," her mother said. "She irons well. She will be so grateful when she learns I want to take her with me to Switzerland, I know she will want to give something in return. She is that type of person."

'While I am only giving brick-bat for brick-bat,' Cañuela thought to herself.

She had reached the bottom of a trunk and, lifting a layer of tissue-paper, she found that there was yet another gown.

She pulled it out.

"I have never seen this before, Mama!"

"I have never worn it," her mother answered.

"But it is beautiful!" Cañuela exclaimed.

She held up a dress of heavy white satin trimmed with ruchings of white tulle, which gave it an ethereal appearance.

"Your father sent for it from Paris for a Ball that was to be given in the President's House," Mrs. Arlington explained in a low voice. "I was just going to put it on when your father came into my room to tell me about the lies and accusations that were circulating about him."

"Oh, Mama! How terrible for you!" Cañuela exclaimed.

"I did not tell you what had happened that night," Mrs. Arlington went on, "because I was so upset, and I did not show you the gown because I had wanted to surprise you."

"I would have been!" Cañuela said. "You used to look like a fairy Princess when you went out to dinner!"

"I think I was also a little ashamed of how much your Papa had spent," Mrs. Arlington said. "He went to such a lot of trouble to buy the gown for me."

"I will leave it here in the trunk," Cañuela said.

"No, no! Take it with you!" Mrs. Arlington begged. "I would love to think of you wearing it. I would like to think that somehow you could go to a Ball at the President's House and to those Palaces on the Plaza St. Martin which all have great Ball-Rooms."

She paused and then went on:

"I shall imagine you waltzing round the room, your hair gleaming under the chandeliers, and being by far the most beautiful person present!"

There was so much emotion in her mother's voice that Cañuela did not argue.

Instead she bent and kissed her.

"I will take it with me, Mama, and hope that your dreams will come true!"

At the same time she told herself:

"There is not a chance of their doing so!"

She knew that her mother still thought of her as a Society girl; someone to be fêted and courted; someone to whom men paid compliments not only because she was beautiful but because of her position in life.

Because she loved her mother she did not wish to disillusion her and explain that there was no chance of her ever again living in that sort of Society.

Because of the shadow of treachery which lay over her father's memory, no man would wish to marry her and revive the terrible publicity, the accusations and speculation.

Cañuela knew that as far as she was concerned the future meant a life of work, of trying to make two ends meet, so that her mother should have some comfort.

Then the existence of an "old maid," perhaps ending up like Miss Graham in one tiny room in a back-street.

Because she was sensible she tried not to dwell on the future but think only of the present.

If she was honest she realised that she had been incredibly lucky to have found employment with someone like Ramón de Lopez.

She might hate him, she might wish to have her revenge for the way he had behaved towards her father, but for the moment he was providing for her mother.

In ordinary circumstances she would have been overwhelmed with gratitude to him, but she told herself now that there was no reason for it.

He was thinking only of himself and his requirements.

When she was of no further use to him he would discard her—perhaps, she thought with a twist of her lips, drop her overboard when the voyages ended!

He was ruthless, egotistical, obstinate, and arrogant to the point where she was crazy to risk her job in answering him back.

She realised that she had been rude this morning.

It would in fact have served her right if he had dispensed with her services immediately.

She had seen the anger in his eyes, and told herself she must be more careful in the future.

There were so many things to do in the next few days that each night when Cañuela got to bed she fell asleep as soon as her head touched the pillow.

She had no time to think; no time to consider.

Dr. Lawson made all the arrangements for her mother to travel with Miss Graham to Switzerland, and they left the day before Cañuela herself was due to leave with Ramón de Lopez.

There were not only things to be done for her mother, there were also so many things required to be done in the office that she felt she would never get through them.

Apart from the letters, papers, and reports she had to organise, there were also innumerable farewell presents to be sent to whole lists of people and, Cañuela found, quite a lot of things to be sent on board before their embarkation.

Amongst them were seventeen corsages made of orchids which all had to be of a different species.

They were to be kept in the refrigerators in the hold until Ramón de Lopez required them.

There was also a collection of the usual French perfume, gloves, and small *objets d'art* which made Cañuela sure that one of the women in whom he was interested was to travel with them.

As she did not see his private letters she had no idea who it was until finally they embarked at Southampton.

Cañuela could not help being amused by the style in which her employer travelled. There were no less than four reserved carriages on the train which left London.

One for Ramón de Lopez, one for the senior members of his staff, one for the valets (he travelled with two), and one for his friends, quite a number of whom it appeared wished to see him off personally.

At Southampton the specially chartered carriages were, with much asthmatic puffs from a little pilot engine which took them in tow, run alongside the ship.

The luggage was seen to by a special Courier, and Cañuela had nothing to do but step up the gang-plank onto the First-Class Deck.

She was standing waiting for someone to tell her where their cabins were situated when Ramón de Lopez, looking extremely distinguished and outstanding even amongst the company of his friends, came aboard.

It seemed as if every member of the crew on the ship wished to bow and scrape at his appearance.

Cañuela realised that they knew him well, as he visited London nearly every year and always used the same Line of Steamships.

He was speaking to the Purser when another passenger arrived.

Cañuela stared.

She was the most beautiful woman she had ever seen!

Dressed elaborately in clothes that would have been more suitable in Hyde Park, she looked like a beautiful butterfly flitting amongst the other passengers.

They all seemed to be in tweed and home-spun, in the drab, unobtrusive colours which English ladies considered correct for travelling abroad.

The newcomer glanced round at the people assembled then gave a little cry of delight.

"Señor Lopez!" she cried and held out her gloved hand with a dramatic gesture.

"Señora Sánchez!" he replied. "This is a surprise and a pleasure!"

"I had no idea you would be travelling home today as I am!" the Señora said. "Now I shall feel safe!"

She glanced at Ramón de Lopez's friends who were all looking at her with undisguised admiration.

"I am so afraid at sea," she said. "Now I know, if the ship should founder, the Señor will save me!"

"We would all be willing to do that!" one of the gentlemen said.

"Then you must all come with us!" the Señora said flirtatiously.

"Your cabin is this way, Miss Gray," a quiet voice said in Cañuela's ear, and she turned to find the Courier beside her.

She followed him, hearing a burst of laughter behind her as something the Señora had said seemed to amuse Ramón de Lopez and his companions.

"Now I know who will receive the orchids," Cañuela said to herself.

It had been quite a clever act on the Señora's part to

pretend surprise at seeing Ramón de Lopez, and he also had acted his part well.

But over the past weeks Cañuela had sent quite a number of bouquets to the Señora, and had also despatched presents to the same lady.

She was certainly beautiful and she could understand Ramón de Lopez's infatuation, if that was the right word for what he felt for her.

The cabins were comfortable and comparatively spacious.

There was a sleeping-cabin for Ramón de Lopez, one of the largest in the ship, the Courier told her, with a Sitting-Room opening out of it.

Cañuela's cabin was discreetly situated further down the corridor.

"The valets will of course be travelling in the next class," the Courier explained, "and I am sure they will get you anything you require, Miss Gray."

"I am used to looking after myself, thank you," Cañuela replied.

"I hope you have a very pleasant voyage."

"Thank you," she replied, and he left her alone in her cabin.

It was comfortable and large enough to accommodate a desk on which her typewriter had been placed, but she had, on her mother's insistence, brought so many things with her that she had a considerable amount of luggage.

She decided that she would unpack at least two of the trunks so that they could be taken away, which would give her more room.

To travel she had worn the same black dress and tight-fitting jacket she wore to go to the office every day.

She had done it deliberately, thinking it would annoy Ramón de Lopez for her to appear in her familiar garb instead of the clothes he imagined he had bought for her.

There was in fact a very pretty travelling-dress and coat of Mrs. Arlington's in her luggage, but some perversity in Cañuela made her decide not to wear it.

She sat down on the bed and thought of her mother

already in Switzerland, and then suddenly the excitement of going abroad, of travelling again, swept over her.

However difficult Ramón de Lopez might be; however much she might hate him and resent him, it was only thanks to his generosity that she was here.

Something young and irrepressible inside her made her feel that this was the beginning of an adventure.

She also both longed and dreaded to see Buenos Aires again.

She had loved the city, but now it was connected in her mind only with the tears they had shed when they realised how badly her father's reputation had been damaged by those who had intrigued against him.

"Poor Papa!" Cañuela said to herself.

Then she remembered his telling her to be proud and put her chin up.

'I will not be beaten,' she thought. 'Perhaps when I reach Argentina I will have the chance of destroying those who destroyed him!'

She might hate Ramón de Lopez but it was nothing like the hatred she felt for Janson Mandell!

He had been the instigator of the whole thing! It was he who had deliberately started the rumours in the first place simply because he had loved her mother, although perhaps love was too decent a word for what he felt for her.

Yet Cañuela could understand that the insult he had received at the hands of her father when he had knocked him down must be revenged.

Janson Mandell had an English name and an English father, but his mother was an Italian from Naples, and to a Neapolitan a vendetta must continue until blood had been shed.

"He won! He succeeded!" Cañuela told herself bitterly. "When Papa died he could not have asked for a better revenge."

Then she told herself that for the next seventeen days while they were at sea she would try not to think of those enemies she might meet again in Argentina.

They would not recognise her, but she could only

hope that somehow her loathing and the curses she heaped upon them would prove disturbing.

In the meantime there was the ship to be explored and the excitement of watching it move away from the dock.

She went to the Upper Deck, thinking it unlikely anyone would notice her there.

She was right.

Most of the people had congregated around the gang-plank, talking to their friends until the last moment when they must go ashore.

The band played, the ship's sirens were sounded, and amid cheers and the waving of hands and handkerchiefs the ship drew away from the Quay to follow a snorting tug which towed it into the deep waters of the Channel.

It was late in the afternoon and Cañuela knew that on the first night at sea dinner would be early.

Most people did not bother to change, with the usual excuse that they had not yet found time to unpack.

Cañuela however decided to put on one of her mother's plainer afternoon-gowns and discard the sombre black which she was sure had annoyed Ramón de Lopez.

She went downstairs to the Dining-Saloon as soon as the dinner-bell rang.

When she said who she was she was shown by the Chief-Steward to a table at one side of the room.

She ate alone and enjoyed watching the other people come in to be conducted, if they were important, with some pomp and ceremony to the Captain's table.

Others were accommodated at the First Officer's table, and the remainder seated anywhere in the Saloon.

Ramón de Lopez was of course at the Captain's table and so was Señora Sánchez.

They entered the Dining-Saloon separately, but apparently by chance they were seated side by side and appeared to have a great deal to say to each other.

Señora Sánchez was wearing a very elaborate evening-gown and seemed quite unperturbed that she was the only woman in the whole Dining-Saloon in full *toilette*.

There was no doubt that she looked superb in blood-red ruby silk which showed off the darkness of her hair and the magnolia quality of her skin.

Her eyes were brilliant and seemed to flash every emotion, whatever she might be saying with her provocative red lips.

Cañuela was not surprised the next morning when Ramón de Lopez told her that a box of orchids was to be sent to the Señora's cabin.

He appeared to be in a good humour and settled down without any personal comments to dictate a report of his visit and the contracts he had made.

A copy, Cañuela learnt, was to be sent to everyone concerned with his visit to England.

He spoke quickly but not at the speed he used when he wished to provoke her.

When after two hours he had finished he said:

"I hope you are comfortable, Miss Gray?"

"Very comfortable, thank you, Señor."

"May I commend you on your gown?"

Cañuela glanced down quickly.

She had put on almost without thinking a dress of deep sapphire-blue crêpe.

It was one of her mother's and exquisitely made, it had the little individual touches characteristic of all of Mrs. Arlington's gowns.

"Thank you, Señor," Cañuela said in a low voice.

"It is too soon to ask if you are enjoying yourself," Ramón de Lopez said. "I will ask you that after we reach Madeira because I have the feeling it is going to be somewhat rough our first days out."

He spoke prophetically.

There was a strong wind and as they moved down the English Channel the sea became more and more turbulent.

Cañuela was a good sailor and she found herself almost the only woman in the Dining-Saloon that evening.

There was no sign of Señora Sánchez for the next four days.

It was difficult to walk about and after she had taken some air and was splashed by a wave while doing it,

Cañuela found it easier to stay reading in her cabin until Ramón de Lopez sent for her.

Every day she was told to send another box of orchids to the Señora.

Cañuela learnt from the Stewardess that she was prostrate with sea-sickness.

"And making a great deal of fuss about it too!" the Stewardess said tartly. "I'm run off my feet with answering that bell."

"Surely she had a lady'smaid with her?" Cañuela asked.

"Lady's-maid!" the Stewardess snorted. "They're as much good as a headache when the sea is rough. They usually succumb before their mistresses!"

The woman looked harassed and Cañuela said:

"If there is anything I can do to help you, let me know. I never feel sea-sick and I am only too willing to help."

"That's very kind of you, Miss," the Stewardess said in surprise. "It's not often anyone offers to give me a hand. We're short of Stewardesses on this trip, I don't know why, but I expect I'll manage!"

Nevertheless because Cañuela was so insistent the Stewardess brought her a passenger's-gown to press and two or three night-gowns to wash.

They were pretty lace-trimmed garments which were no trouble and the Stewardess was overwhelmingly grateful.

"I've never known anyone as kind as you, Miss, and that's a fact," she said.

"I have little to do and you have too much!" Cañuela replied. "It is only fair that we should share it between us."

Ramón de Lopez worked in bursts of energy.

Sometimes he gave her two or three hours' dictation; at others she would go practically a whole day and not hear from him.

It appeared that he had a great deal of reading to do, which she realised from the number of books he had lying about his Sitting-Room.

They were mostly political and she thought that perhaps her father had been right when he said he was aiming at the Presidency.

Although she hated him she had to admit he would be a good President.

The Argentines liked sportsmen. They liked their leaders to be athletic, ready to be in the saddle all day without feeling tired, and to play superb polo.

She knew that Ramón de Lopez was one of the best players in the world.

That he could also be clever and knowledgeable about his country's finances and a brilliant negotiator was an extra bonus one did not always find in one man!

The sea was subsiding and the sun shining when they reached the Island of Madeira, which was the only port of call between England and Buenos Aires.

Cañuela had only heard about Madeira, since on her other trips to South America they had always gone via Lisbon.

As the ship anchored in the Bay of Funchal the Island seemed enchanted as it sloped steeply from the pebbly beach to the cloud-capped hills.

Everything was green behind the buildings with their white, yellow, or light-blue walls, red roofs and green shutters.

Before the ship had put down the anchor Cañuela had recognised banana trees, palms, and a profusion of vines.

The moment the ship hove to, a whole crowd of small boats put off from the shore.

There were vendors selling the Island's fruit, baskets, straw-work, holding up their wares and bargaining with the passengers leaning from the decks.

There were swaggering Customs Officers in uniforms of black, white, and gold, and boat-loads of practically nude boy-divers beseeching the passengers to throw coins for which they were prepared to dive deep into the clear green water.

Cañuela watched them with delight.

Their agility and dexterity made her want to clap her hands as never a coin escaped them. Occasionally two or three could be seen struggling beneath the water to obtain possession of a shilling.

As soon as the customary preliminaries were over the passengers were permitted to go ashore. Feeling sure that Ramón de Lopez would not need her, Cañuela was one of the first to disembark.

The steep paths paved with smooth grey pebbles were not easy to walk on.

The constant traffic of log-sledges, guided by drivers with long poles, had worn them as smooth as glass so that it was difficult to secure a foot-hold.

But outside the town there were carriages for hire, if one could afford them!

Tourists could drive amongst the rich foliage sloping down from the mountains and see the colourful flowers, especially the arum lilies, which grew wild all over the Island.

Cañuela had agreed after a great deal of argument with her mother to take ten pounds with her on the voyage.

"You must have some money, dearest," Mrs. Arlington had said. "There are people you might wish to tip. Besides, you cannot ask Señor Lopez—after all he has given you—for the collection in Church or a penny for a reel of cotton!"

Because it really worried her mother, Cañuela took ten pounds out of the three hundred Ramón de Lopez had given her, and thought that if she had anything left over on the return journey she would bring her mother a present.

She had no intention of frittering away her money, so she walked up the slippery grey pebbles until she reached the dusty roads. Then she climbed up the hill-side.

She knew that if she climbed high enough above the harbour and town she would have a magnificent view.

She was not mistaken.

The air was cool although the sun was hot, and the flowers and tropical vegetation were so lovely that the effort was well worthwhile.

Down below her the market-place looked like a child's toy, and she thought how wise she had been to avoid the temptation which every market imposes upon those who visit them.

She could see some of the passengers from the ship setting off in log-sledges. Then she noticed two of the passengers driving in an open carriage along the road which looked like a ribbon beneath her.

It was not hard to recognise the pink dress Señora Sánchez was wearing.

Cañuela had seen her on deck watching the diving-boys and thought that she looked like a rose.

Her hat, which was trimmed with flowers, was tied under her chin with ribbons, and despite the fact that Mrs. Arlington would have thought it bad taste, the Señora was glittering with diamonds.

"I wonder if he is in love with her?" Cañuela questioned.

She could see their two heads bent towards each other far away below her and she wondered if they were holding hands.

When they could stop the carriage they would doubtless wander away through the trees and their embraces could become more intimate.

"As she is a married woman she should behave better!" Cañuela told herself sternly.

Señor Juan Sánchez was a member of the Government.

When Cañuela had last been in Buenos Aires he had been President of the Board of Trade, but she had learnt from the newspapers which she read in London that he was now the Minister of Finance.

She recalled him as rather a florid man, quick-tempered and somewhat aggressive.

She had the feeling that her father had never liked him, although he had quite a number of dealings with him in one way or another.

Anyway the Señor had certainly found himself a very beautiful wife!

Cañuela did not feel that he would be very pleased if he knew she was carrying on a flirtation with Ramón de Lopez, who was as notorious in Argentina for his love-affairs as for his horsemanship.

Watching them driving along the twisting road, Cañuela noticed behind them another carriage, which contained only one man.

She thought it odd that one of the passengers should go for a drive by himself.

Then she remembered a conversation she had had the day before with the Stewardess.

"There is a man I am always seeing in the corridor," Cañuela had said. "He is small and dark and has a scar on his cheek. I never see him in the Dining-Saloon, so I rather suspect he is not a First-Class passenger."

"He is not indeed," the Stewardess replied. "I know the man you mean and I have told the Head-Steward about him."

"Do you think he is a thief?" Cañuela asked.

"I don't think so," the Stewardess answered, "but I would not be surprised if he was a Journalist."

"What makes you think he might be working for a newspaper?" Cañuela asked.

"Well, he is very inquisitive, for one thing," the Stewardess replied. "He has asked me questions about nearly everyone on this floor."

"About me?" Cañuela asked, having a sudden fear that her identity might have been discovered.

"No, not about you, Miss Gray," the Stewardess answered, "but he is certainly interested in your employer."

"I wonder why," Cañuela remarked.

Then she thought that the man might be connected with a rival firm which Ramón de Lopez was not representing.

She was well aware that all the concessions and contracts made in England were to be kept secret until he reached Argentina.

She was quite certain that it was the same man even at this distance.

She recognised the way he held his head and the rather strange-shaped hat he wore. She had seen him holding it in his hand when he was walking down the corridor.

Then suddenly Cañuela knew the answer.

The man was not a Journalist but a detective!

She knew how fanatically jealous Argentines could be about their wives, and Juan Sánchez was just the type of man who would, undoubtedly with reason, wish to know what his wife was doing when he was not with her.

High on the hill, sitting amongst the wild lilies, Cañuela wondered if here was her revenge.

If the detective reported, as he surely would, that Ramón de Lopez was having an affair with Señora Sánchez, her husband would challenge him.

There might be a duel, or he might expose the guilty couple in a manner which would ensure they were ostracised by the more respectable members of Society.

It would certainly put a stop to Ramón de Lopez's ambitions to become President.

Argentines admired a man who was full-blooded. They expected him to have mistresses. They expected him to be gay and raffish.

But to tamper with the affections of another man's wife was a very different matter.

A wife was a man's possession; his chattel! Just as a horse-thief was punished by hanging, it was not considered murder to shoot down in cold blood an adulterer.

'This is my revenge,' Cañuela thought.

Then she knew she could not let it happen.

It was one thing to revenge herself on Ramón de Lopez, quite another to see him defamed!

Cañuela walked back to the harbour. A launch took her to the ship.

It was over an hour later before Ramón de Lopez and Señora Sánchez came aboard. The man with the scar on his face followed in the next boat.

Cañuela waited until she was sure that Ramón de Lopez would be alone in his Sitting-Room.

The anchor had already been drawn up and the ship was in the process of sailing.

Many people were on deck, watching the ship move out of the Bay, but he was too experienced a traveller to be interested.

When Cañuela entered the cabin he looked up with what she thought was an expression of pleasure.

"I was just going to send for you, Miss Gray," he said. "I have one or two items to add to that report we did yesterday."

She hesitated, but he did not notice it and went on:

"Did you go ashore?"

"Yes."

"It is a very beautiful Island."

"Very beautiful indeed, Señor."

She did not sit down and he looked at her with a question in his eyes.

"What is it?" he asked.

"You were followed this afternoon," she said. "There is a man who has been making enquiries about you. He is constantly in the corridor outside."

Ramón de Lopez was still.

"What do you think he wants?" he asked after a moment.

"That is not for me to say," Cañuela replied. "I merely thought you should know."

"Why have you bothered to tell me this?" he asked.

She felt that the question was embarrassing. Then she told the truth.

"A scandal would . . . harm you."

"Surely that would please you. You have shown your dislike of me very clearly, Miss Gray."

"You knew . . . that and yet you . . . brought me on this voyage?" Cañuela asked.

"I need you, as you well know. At the same time I am curious as to the reason for your attitude."

There was silence and then Cañuela said:

"I think, Señor, we should . . . start work."

"I want an answer to my question," he said. "Why are you not prepared to stand by and see me discredited? I am sure, Miss Gray, you are far too intelligent not to realise what the man actually is."

"It is not my . . . concern."

"But you have made my reputation your concern."

He paused to add:

"Is it perhaps because you are grateful to me?"

There was no doubt of the irony in his voice and Cañuela said after a moment:

"No, it is not . . . that."

"Then I would like an explanation."

There was silence and then Cañuela said hesitatingly:

"Someone . . . whose judgment I respected . . . once said that you would make . . . a good . . . President of Argentina."

"Then you had heard of me before?" he said sharply.

Cañuela blushed.

She might have known that he would not let a point like that escape him.

"You are well-known, Señor," she murmured.

"But hardly outside Argentina."

She did not answer and after a moment he said:

"And you agree with your informant?"

"Yes."

"And yet personally you hate me."

"Y-yes."

She spoke the monosyllable with difficulty.

"You are at least honest, Miss Gray. Will you tell me why?"

"No!"

"Why not?"

"I am under no obligation to do so, Señor. May I remind you that I am here to work for you? My feelings, whatever they may be, can be of no interest to you whatsoever."

"Strangely enough, they do interest me," Ramón de Lopez said, "and frankly, Miss Gray, I find it infuriating to work with anyone whose whole attitude is one of dislike and whose every spoken word sounds as if it had come from a *frigorifico!*"

Cañuela said nothing and after a moment he ejaculated as if he could not help himself:

"Have you nothing to say? God knows it is maddening to talk to a woman who makes herself out to be a Sphynx or an enigma!"

"I am not here to talk, Señor."

"But I want to talk to you," Ramón de Lopez said almost like a spoilt child. "If I am to be denied the pleasure of the Señora's company for the rest of the voyage, then I shall have to content myself with conversing with you!"

"I am sorry you must suffer such hardship!" Cañuela said sarcastically.

Ramón de Lopez looked at her for a moment and then he said:

"I do not know where you were brought up, Miss Gray, but it is obvious you were allowed your own way, which is a mistake for a young woman. I can only hope that one of your men-friends, although you say you have none, will one day give you the spanking you deserve!"

Again Cañuela did not reply and after a moment he said angrily:

"Well, sit down! At least you are more or less human when I am working with you and, if I have to thaw out a *frigorifico,* we might as well start with the one contact we have with each other!"

Cañuela sat down on the hard chair and opened her note-book.

"I am ready, Señor," she said in a meek tone which she hoped would infuriate him.

Behind her spectacles her eyes were triumphant!

She had got under his skin!

She had succeeded in breaking through his arrogant self-satisfaction!

At the same time she had saved him!

FOUR

Cañuela was changing for dinner when there was a knock at the door and the Stewardess came in, carrying in her hand a box.

"With the compliments of Señor Ramón de Lopez!"

Cañuela looked at the box incredulously.

She could hardly believe that he would send her a box of the orchids which he had bought for Señora Sánchez.

For a moment she contemplated sending them back to him; and then she realised that there were two reasons why he might have ordered the corsage to be brought to her.

First, which she could hardly credit, he was so ingenuous as to believe that she would take them as a compliment for having warned him about the detective.

Secondly, that he was deliberately distracting the detective's attention from Señora Sánchez to herself.

It seemed to Cañuela on reflection that the latter was the most likely reason, but at the same time it was still an insult.

"They're very beautiful!" the Stewardess said wistfully.

"Let me give them to you," Cañuela said.

The Stewardess looked at her in surprise.

"I do not like orchids," Cañuela explained.

"And I'd have no chance of wearing them on board," the Stewardess laughed.

"Perhaps there is someone who would be grateful for them," Cañuela suggested.

"Well, as a matter of fact, there is," the Stewardess replied. "There is a lady at the far end of the corridor who has not been well the whole voyage. Señora Pinto has three children and I really think a gift like this would cheer her up."

"Then please take them to her," Cañuela said.

"They would go nicely with your gown," the Stewardess remarked, looking at the very pretty dress Cañuela had just put on.

"As I have said, I dislike orchids. They are far too exotic and opulent for me in my position."

"I think you are being over-modest, Miss Gray," the Stewardess smiled, then added:

"I have something very interesting to tell you."

"What is it?" Cañuela enquired.

"You remember that man you were talking about who was always lurking about in the corridors?"

"Yes, I remember him."

"Well, I spoke about him to the Head-Steward, and he spoke to the Purser, who told him to stay down in the Second-Class where he belonged."

"That is a good thing . . ." Cañuela started to say, but she was interrupted as the Stewardess went on:

"So what do you think has happened? He's changed his ticket!"

"You mean he has paid extra to come up on this deck?" Cañuela asked.

"Exactly!" the Stewardess answered. "I suppose he did not think the Second-Class was good enough for him, or else he did not have enough people to talk about down there!"

"Yes, I expect that is the reason," Cañuela agreed.

She thought as she went below to the Dining-Saloon that it was fortunate she had noticed the detective following Señor Lopez and his beautiful companion when they had been driving round the Island.

Had she not climbed so high up the mountain-side, it would have been quite easy to miss what was happening, and with the detective in the same corridor there was no doubt that but for her having warned Señor Lopez there would have been plenty to report to his employer.

Cañuela was down to dinner later than was usual and

the Dining-Saloon seemed almost full as she walked to her table.

She noticed that Señora Sánchez was already seated at the Captain's table, looking lovely and voluptuous in an elaborate gown of green silk which matched the enormous necklace of emeralds round her white neck.

Cañuela had always admired the beauty of the Argentine women who were mature by the time they were fifteen, yet often they deteriorated early in life.

There was no doubt that Señora Sánchez was at the very height of her beauty, and Cañuela could understand that it would be hard for any man to resist the invitation in her dark eyes and provocative red lips.

Cañuela had no sooner ordered her meal than she saw Ramón de Lopez enter the Dining-Saloon.

He walked through the crowded tables to where the Captain was sitting with all the important passengers round him, but instead of taking his usual seat he bent forward to talk earnestly in the Captain's ear for some seconds.

To Cañuela's astonishment he then walked to her table and sat down on the chair opposite her.

She saw that he carried some papers in his hand.

"I have explained to the Captain," he said, "that I have received some extremely important cablegrams which must be dealt with immediately. I have therefore asked him to excuse me from sitting at his table so that I can discuss business matters with you."

Cañuela could not help feeling that Señora Sánchez would be very surprised at what had happened.

In fact from where she was sitting she could see the Señora looking towards Ramón de Lopez with what was not only a puzzled but an angry expression on her face.

"Were there really any cables?" Cañuela asked.

"Fortunately several, to give credibility to my story," he replied, "but they are not of any particular importance or urgency."

He smiled.

"Nevertheless if you are to support my contention, and I cannot believe you would let me down, you must talk to me. We cannot sit in silence like a bored married couple who have run out of conversation!"

Cañuela could not help a faint smile and Ramón de Lopez took a cablegram from the top of the pile of papers and handed it to her.

"Try and look as if the English have ordered another million tons of frozen meat!" he said. "Or, if you prefer, let us face the fact that Argentina has gone bankrupt and we must discuss how to ride the economic crisis!"

Because she felt that she must take part in this play-acting, Cañuela read the cablegram, which was one she had already deciphered earlier in the day, and then handed it back to him.

He gave her another and she went through the same action.

When he had ordered what he wished to eat, the wine-steward handed him the *Carte des Vins*.

"Do you prefer white wine or red?" Señor Lopez asked Cañuela.

"I am drinking water," she answered.

"A vintage I have never recommended on a Steamship!" he answered.

He ordered a bottle of Piesporter, which Cañuela remembered had been one of her father's favourite Moselles. Because she felt she would like to taste it again she did not protest when the steward filled her glass.

"May I compliment you on your gown?" Ramón de Lopez asked.

"Perhaps I should compliment you, Señor!" Cañuela replied, remembering that he thought he had paid for it.

"I feel perhaps it is lacking in ornamentation," he said. "Did you not receive my orchids?"

"Yes," Cañuela replied.

There was a pause and then he asked:

"Is there any reason why you are not wearing them?"

"Yes . . . two," Cañuela answered stiffly.

"And what are they?"

She considered refusing to answer his question, but because his attitude was almost one of an interrogator and because she still felt insulted by his gift a sudden anger made her reply:

"I am prepared, Señor, to play Chaperon to a frustrated Romeo, but not to understudy the part of Juliet!"

Even as Cañuela spoke she realised how rude she sounded.

She saw an expression of astonishment in Ramón de Lopez's eyes and then a gleam of fire as he replied:

"You are certainly, Miss Gray, approaching precipitously near to that spanking I said you needed!"

"Brutal strength is hardly a subtle or civilised method of argument, Señor!"

His lips tightened for a moment, almost as if he repressed a smile, and then he answered:

"But where women and horses are concerned it is often necessary."

"Your stable, Señor, has my sympathy."

As she spoke Cañuela lifted her chin.

She wished she was not wearing spectacles so that he could see the defiance in her eyes. Then Ramón de Lopez said more quietly and with what she thought was an effort at control:

"You said there were two reasons for not wearing my orchids. What was the second?"

"I do not like orchids."

There was a smile at the corner of his lips, as if he had expected a much more complicated explanation. Then he said:

"I have heard that women resemble flowers. You are right! The orchid is not the flower for you."

He paused and asked:

"Have you any idea what would be appropriate?"

"Why not a snap-dragon?" Cañuela asked.

Ramón de Lopez gave a low laugh of genuine amusement.

"You are always unpredictable, Miss Gray!" he exclaimed. "I cannot imagine any other woman saying such a thing!"

The steward served another course and when the man had withdrawn Ramón de Lopez said:

"I had never before realised how expressive a woman's lips could be!"

Cañuela glanced at him suspiciously.

She was well aware that he was making conversation. At the same time this was not the sort of topic she had expected.

"Always before," he went on, "I have watched emotions betrayed by the eyes, but as I cannot see yours I find I am learning from your mouth what you are feeling."

Instinctively Cañuela pressed her lips together.

"Now you are worried," Ramón de Lopez said quietly. "You are afraid I will get to know those things you are keeping secret from me."

"You are trying to embarrass me," Cañuela said accusingly.

"Why should you be embarrassed, unless you are ashamed of what you are hiding?"

"I do not wish to talk about myself, Señor."

"But I wish to talk about you. You have constituted yourself my Guardian Angel. Now you must take the consequences."

"I see I made a mistake!"

"Think how proud of me you will be when I am elected President! 'I did it!' you will say to yourself!"

"You are very confident, Señor. Pride goes before a fall!"

"You had your chance, Miss Gray."

"I shall doubtless regret not taking it!"

Another course interrupted their conversation.

While they were eating it, Ramón de Lopez said with what seemed a change of mood:

"Is the spy here in this room?"

"Yes. He is sitting by the door."

Cañuela told him what the Stewardess had said about the man changing his Second-Class ticket.

She saw that Ramón de Lopez was thinking over the information, then he said:

"How can I warn Señora Sánchez of this without being alone with her?"

Cañuela thought for a moment, then she suggested slowly:

"I could ask the Stewardess to tell her lady's-maid that the man has been making enquiries about her."

Ramón de Lopez gave a sigh of relief.

"If you will do that I will be most grateful."

There was silence and then Cañuela said:

"I have a suggestion to make to you, Señor."

"What is it?"

"It may sound . . . impertinent."

"I will not put any construction on it that you do not intend."

"Then why in the days that are left of the voyage do you not set down on paper your ideas for the future of Argentina?"

He did not speak but she knew he was listening intently as she went on:

"It often seems as if Government Departments work individually, without having a consolidated National Policy."

"That is true."

"But if there were an over-all plan of development, which there has not been for the last few years in Argentina, then with her enormous natural resources she could expand as she has never done before."

Cañuela spoke very seriously.

When she finished Ramón de Lopez said with a note of incredulity in his voice:

"How on earth can you know this?"

Cañuela started.

She had been so immersed in her idea that she had not realised that from her own point of view she had said too much.

Quickly, to cover her slip, she said:

"I . . . I . . . read many of the . . . books and magazines which were lying about in the office in London."

Ramón de Lopez gave her a sharp glance as if he suspected that this was untrue.

But he was so intrigued by her suggestion that he began to elaborate on it.

Then he said:

"I think what we must do is write a pamphlet with facts and figures which can be distributed to every member of the Government."

"That is what I hoped you would say."

He raised his eye-brows.

"That is hardly the right sentiment for an enemy, Miss Gray."

There was a faint smile on Cañuela's lips as she replied:

"In an emergency it is a question of 'every hand to the pumps'!"

Ramón de Lopez threw back his head and this time his laughter rang out unrestrainedly.

For the next ten days Cañuela worked harder than she had ever before worked in her life.

She was to learn that once Ramón de Lopez was enthusiastic about something, it occupied all his thoughts and imagination.

She found it difficult to persuade him that he must give her time to set down in type what he dictated to her in shorthand.

Only because he needed exercise would he break off after a long session of dictation to give her a chance to return to her own cabin to type it back.

There were also cipher cables to be sent, and more than once when the day was ended Cañuela thought she was certainly earning her money and she did not feel so guilty in taking such a large sum from her employer.

At the same time she was fascinated.

She found, as she had expected, that Ramón de Lopez had not only a comprehensive grasp of the financial position in Argentina, but some revolutionary ideas of how the whole country could go forward into the future.

"I believe," he said to Cañuela and also in his report, "that our prosperity is indivisibly tied up with Great Britain."

The British Government had already invested a great deal of money in Argentina but private investors had been disillusioned and shocked by a crisis concerning the Baring Bank which had taken place four years earlier.

There had also been rising inflation, demonstrations in the streets, illegal issues of currency, and the bankruptcy of several railways.

These difficulties and a number of others had obviously made investors wary, but it was essential, if Argentina was to expand, that she should be backed by British Banking-Enterprises.

"What is encouraging," Ramón de Lopez said, "is that the British community is absorbing an increasing tide of Argentine products."

"But it is not enough, I suppose?" Cañuela said.

"Not nearly," he answered, "and at the moment we are achieving expansion under the difficult conditions of falling prices, which means that the terms of trade are unfavourable to Argentina."

"But you still have low labour costs," Cañuela said, "and an abundance of virgin land."

Again he glanced at her as though he was surprised at her knowledge, but he was too interested in developing his own theme to challenge her as he might have done on another occasion.

"What we really want is a war!" he said.

Cañuela looked at him in horror.

"In Argentina?"

"No, of course not!" he replied, "but somewhere else in the world. A war demands vast expenditure, and we could supply horses, hides, beef, mutton, wheat, and wool."

"I cannot help hoping you will sell these in peacetime also," Cañuela said.

"I hope so too," Ramón de Lopez replied, "but war would accelerate the golden years which I am absolutely convinced lie ahead."

Sometimes he seemed impatient when it was time to dress for dinner or even go to the Dining-Saloon for luncheon, but at others he would be considerate.

"Am I driving you too hard?" he would ask. "Forgive me. It is your own fault for inspiring me."

"Have I done that?" Cañuela asked.

"Who else?" he replied. "I had not thought of this until you suggested it."

He rose to walk across the cabin.

"Who said that everything is for the best in the best of all possible worlds?"

"Voltaire, I think."

"He spoke very truly where I am concerned," Ramón de Lopez said. "If it had not been for you and what we might call an 'amatory crisis,' this report would never have been written!"

"You think it is really important?" Cañuela asked.

"I believe in it!" he said, "and I will make the Government believe in it too!"

He spoke with a quiet determination which made Cañuela feel that he would get his own way.

Then he added:

"I told you that you would be proud of me."

She thought of his words when dinner was over and she returned to her own cabin.

Ever since they had left Madeira and the detective had moved into the Dining-Saloon, Ramón de Lopez had not returned to the Captain's table.

Every night he brought with him to Cañuela's table papers and sometimes books.

Occasionally they made a pretence of consulting them and sometimes scribbled a few words on a piece of paper as if making notes.

They had an audience to watch what they did; for Cañuela was well aware that Señora Sánchez's eyes were on them every evening.

She looked sulky and resentful, like a child who has been deprived of a toy.

It was however a satisfaction to think that the detective was wasting his time and his employer's money, for there was nothing he could possibly report.

Ramón de Lopez did not retire after dinner as Cañuela did, but he went to the Card-Room and his phenomenal luck was soon the talk of the ship.

"The Señor won an immense amount of gold last night," the gossiping Stewardess would tell Cañuela. "At this rate half the passengers will step off at Buenos Aires with empty pockets and debts that'll hang round their necks like millstones!"

"I expect they can afford it!" Cañuela said.

"That's a fact," the Stewardess answered. "From all I hear there are a dozen millionaires at least on the First-Class Deck!"

Even if Cañuela had wished to mix with the other

passengers, which she did not, there was no chance of her doing so.

When she was not with Ramón de Lopez she was typing.

Because she too was enthusiastic about their work she had to force herself to walk round the deck in the morning and evening.

She would lean over the rail as the weather grew warmer to watch the dolphins desporting themselves in the blue sea, or just feel content to have the sunshine warm on her skin.

They were getting nearer to the end of their voyage every day and Cañuela began to wonder how she would feel when it was over.

It was almost as if she were living in a tiny island alone with Ramón de Lopez.

It was hard for her to keep up her cold reserve and quite impossible to continue to answer him in monosyllables.

He would often stop dictating to discuss a point with her, not only asking her opinion, but finding out if what he was saying would have the impact that he wished it to have on those who would listen to his ideas.

Sometimes she would disagree with him.

Then they would argue fiercely and Cañuela would wonder afterwards why she did not let him have his own way without opposition.

What did it matter to her whether his report was a success or not?

Then she told herself that she was doing it for the country she had always loved and for which her father had given so many years of his life.

She had only to think of her father for it to hurt her unbearably to know that Ramón de Lopez had let him down when he had most need of his friendship.

It was at these moments she would say to herself again:

"I hate him!"

But somehow the words seemed to have lost the passionate emotion they had expressed when she was in London.

Every day she wrote part of a letter to her mother,

keeping it almost like a diary so that Mrs. Arlington would know exactly what had happened to her since they parted.

But Cañuela was finding it more and more difficult to describe her relationship with her employer.

It was difficult to go on being as cold as he had accused her of being; of showing him her indifference or even the hatred which she knew was provocative.

She had not realised before how fascinating it was to talk to a man. She had never in her life had luncheon or dinner with any man alone except her father.

She had not since she was grown up been in the company of a gentleman and an intelligent one at that!

She found her own mind expanding. She found that she had new ideas and a deeper knowledge of the history of the period than she had realised.

She found too that even when the conversation became personal there was something exhilarating and exciting in the cut and thrust of their repartee.

They were duelling with each other; fighting a battle in which neither was the victor, and when they rested their weapons it was with the knowledge that they would take them up again the next day.

After a long session when the report was nearly finished Ramón de Lopez ordered champagne for dinner.

"We both deserve it!" he said. "You are a slave-driver, Miss Gray! I have never spent so many hours of sheer mental activity as I have on this voyage!"

"But there is something to show for it," Cañuela suggested.

"Thanks to you," he replied.

He raised his glass.

"To the most efficient secretary in the world."

He drank a little and raised it again.

"To a woman with a mysterious and intriguing mouth!"

The words came as a surprise and Cañuela felt the colour rising in her cheeks.

"Do not spoil it," she begged.

"What am I spoiling?" he asked. "An office relationship?"

She did not answer and he went on:

"Can you really think of yourself as an ordinary employee, a typist whom I engaged casually from an Agency?"

Still Cañuela did not answer and he said:

"We have progressed much further than that, you and I. But you are still hiding something from me. You are still a woman with a secret!"

Cañuela put down her glass.

"I think, Señor," she said, "that if those last drafts are to be finished before we dock, I should go back to my cabin. I have at least two hours' work before I go to bed."

Ramón de Lopez's eyes were twinkling as he replied:

"Still running away? From what and to whom?"

"There is no answer to that question."

"Only because you will not give me one."

"That is something I shall never do," she answered.

She rose to her feet so that he was forced to rise to his, picked up a pile of papers that he had brought with him to the table, and went from the Saloon.

When she reached her cabin she undressed and put on her night-gown and a pretty muslin wrapper trimmed with lace which had belonged to her mother.

Then she brushed her hair.

She had learned that if she did not do this early in the evening she was usually too tired after she had finished work.

She had promised her mother years ago when she was only a child that she would brush her hair at least a hundred strokes every night.

"Your hair is so beautiful, dearest," Mrs. Arlington had said. "It is not the colour of mine or your father's but of your grandmother's. She was acclaimed one of the great beauties when Queen Victoria first came to the throne."

"I cannot believe she was more beautiful than you, Mama."

"Much, much more lovely," Mrs. Arlington said. "All the great artists wanted to paint her. Her portrait appeared every year at the Royal Academy Exhibition and it is said that the young Queen was jealous of her, which was not surprising!"

"And was my grandfather handsome?"

"I thought until I saw your Papa that he was the most handsome man in the world," Mrs. Arlington replied.

There was a pain in her voice which told Cañuela that her mother had loved her father deeply.

"Did you mind leaving home to marry Papa?"

"I hated to deceive my father and I had always wanted to do what he wished," Mrs. Arlington replied. "But love is something none of us can control."

"You mean when you fell in love with Papa no-one else mattered?"

"No-one!" Mrs. Arlington said. "That is what happens when one is in love. It is overwhelming, irresistible. I was swept off my feet, bewitched, dazzled, and I knew . . ."

She paused and Cañuela asked:

"What did you know, Mama?"

"I knew," Mrs. Arlington said softly, "that without your father I had no wish to go on living."

She gave a little sigh and said with a smile:

"That is what happens when one is in love, Cañuela! There is only one person left in the whole world. Everything and everyone else vanishes. He is a part of you and you are a part of him and any sacrifice is worthwhile! Then you know you are in love!"

'I hope that I shall feel like that one day,' Cañuela thought at the time.

Now she told herself that as far as she was concerned her life meant work and nothing else.

At the same time, however much she might accept the cold austerity of such a prospect, she could not help being glad that her hair released from its tight bun rippled over her shoulders in great, gleaming red-gold waves.

It was a relief to be able to take off her glasses. At least she could type without wearing them. It had become a strain to see her own shorthand through the tinted lenses, and they were also heavy on the bridge of her small, straight nose.

Cañuela had reached one hundred strokes of her brush when there was a knock at the door, and when she called out, "Come in," the Stewardess put her head inside.

"Would you be an angel and help me, Miss Gray?" she asked.

"Of course," Cañuela answered. "What do you want me to do?"

"Could you give Señora Pinto's baby his feed?" the Stewardess asked. "You remember, that's the lady to whom you sent the orchids?"

"Yes, of course I remember," Cañuela replied.

The Stewardess came further into the cabin and Cañuela saw that she was carrying a small baby wrapped up in a white shawl.

"His mother is not well tonight," the Stewardess explained. "When I had the milk ready she did not seem to have enough strength to give it to the child."

"I will do it," Cañuela said with a smile.

"I wouldn't ask you, Miss Gray," the Stewardess went on, "if there weren't half a dozen bells ringing for me and two of the other Stewardesses have gone to their supper. Heaven knows what's keeping them! I'm all on my own!"

"Do not worry," Cañuela said, "he seems a good baby."

"He is when he's not hungry!" the Stewardess replied.

As if he realised that this was his cue, the baby started to cry.

Cañuela took him in her arms and the Stewardess gave her the bottle and vanished.

At one time or another in her life Cañuela had had a lot to do with babies.

When she and her parents were travelling there were always Diplomats' children to be looked after or played with. Mrs. Arlington was someone to whom everyone turned in times of trouble.

Once when there had been an epidemic of measles in Lisbon they had no less than three small children staying with them, so that they should not be infected by their brothers and sisters who had already succumbed to the complaint.

The baby sucked at his bottle greedily and when it was empty fell asleep in Cañuela's arms.

He was a pretty child with a magnolia skin, an obvious inheritance of his Spanish ancestry, and wisps of dark hair were just beginning to grow on his well-shaped head.

Cañuela rocked him gently and found herself wondering if she would ever hold a child of her own in her arms.

She knew that as she had planned her life there was no chance of motherhood and yet something within her rebelled at the thought.

She wanted children.

She wanted to love them and for them to love her. Then she realised that this also included the love of a man.

She wondered what it would be like to love a man in the way her mother had described; to know that nothing else mattered except that she should be with him.

With what was almost a physical pain she knew that no man would ever feel that way for her. How could they?

She was the daughter of a man accused of treason—a man who many people believed had been a traitor to his country and to his profession.

"It is not fair!" Cañuela wanted to cry out.

There was a knock at the door.

"Come in," she said, knowing that it was the Stewardess.

As the door opened Cañuela looked down at the baby.

"He has been very good," she said, "and as soon as he finished his bottle he went fast asleep!"

There was no answer and she raised her head.

It was not the Stewardess who stood just inside the door but Ramón de Lopez!

Cañuela felt as if she could not move.

He seemed very large and very tall in the cabin; in fact he seemed overwhelming as he stood looking at her.

Then she was conscious that she was wearing only a muslin wrap over her night-gown, that her hair was falling over her shoulders, and her eyes were not covered by the disfiguring spectacles.

To Ramón de Lopez her grey-green eyes were enormous in her small face.

Because she was so surprised at his appearance in her cabin her lips parted and yet it seemed for the moment as if she could hardly breathe.

There was a long, long silence.

"So that is why you hide your eyes!" he said at length in a low voice.

Cañuela forced herself to answer him.

"What is . . . it you . . . want?"

She was unable to move because of the child in her arms.

She was also, for some reason she did not understand, unable to take her eyes from Ramón de Lopez.

"I came," he said after a moment's hesitation, as if trying to collect his thoughts, "to ask you for the code-book which you took with you with the papers you carried from the Dining-Saloon."

Cañuela did not answer and he said as if in explanation:

"You told me you would be working for another two hours."

"Y-yes . . . yes, of course," Cañuela said. "I was . . . just going to . . . start."

"Why do you disguise yourself?" he asked, then added: "Perhaps that is a stupid question!"

"It was . . . the only way I . . . could be . . . safe!"

"I can understand that."

In some extraordinary way Cañuela felt as though they were speaking to each other not in the words they were using but in a very different manner.

She had the crazy idea that they were talking across eternity and they had met again after centuries of time.

Then with an effort she stammered:

"T-the . . . the c-code-book is . . . on my . . . d-desk."

As she spoke she looked down at the child sleeping against her breast and her hair fell forward like a curtain to hide her face.

She heard Ramón de Lopez take a step towards the desk. There was a rustle of papers and he said in a carefully controlled voice:

"Good-night, Miss Gray! I regret having had to disturb you."

Cañuela did not answer.

She only felt as if something strange, something momentous, had occurred.

It was as if the curtain had risen on the second act of a play and she was not certain what was going to happen.

She told herself she was being imaginative.

What did it matter if Ramón de Lopez had seen her without her spectacles? As her employer it could hardly make any difference to their relationship.

She had told him she hated him, and if she continued to irritate him she knew that everything would go on as before.

At the same time she was apprehensive.

The following morning Cañuela took care to be already in Ramón de Lopez's Sitting-Room when he returned from his exercise.

She had felt as she dressed that it would be impossible for her to walk in and know that his eyes were on her; that he was longing to ask her curious questions for which she had no answers.

Instead she arranged herself in her usual seat, placing the typed papers already completed on a table at her side.

She also arranged the pile of books they had been using for research, and opened them at the appropriate pages.

He entered the cabin and unaccountably she found her heart beating faster.

'I'm being foolish!' she chided herself. 'He had no right to come to my cabin and if he is a gentleman he will not mention it again.'

Ramón de Lopez sat down in his usual chair.

He studied her for a moment and then said quietly:

"You know as well as I do that those spectacles are bad for your eye-sight. When we are alone there is no longer any point in your wearing them."

"I prefer to wear them," Cañuela replied.

She did not know why but she felt that they were a life-line to which she must cling.

"That is illogical!" Ramón de Lopez said. "You wore them for a reason which no longer exists."

He paused and went on:

"I realise that it would be impossible for a woman with looks like yours to work in an ordinary office without facing intolerable insults from men who would be unable to leave her alone."

Cañuela did not raise her eyes and he said:

"But you have made it very clear that you hate me and I assure you that I am extremely conscious of my short-comings where you are concerned. I therefore suggest that you discard what is now a very ineffective disguise!"

For a moment Cañuela hesitated.

She had grown to feel that her spectacles were an armour and she would feel vulnerable without them. Then she told herself that his argument was irrefutable.

What was more, to refuse might make him think she was afraid that he might make advances towards her.

It was a two-edged argument and she thought it would be more dignified if she acquiesced gracefully rather than have him continue, as she was certain he would, to argue with her about it.

With a somewhat dramatic gesture she took the spectacles from her eyes.

"Very well, Señor," she said, "but I shall continue to wear what you call 'my disguise' outside this cabin. My mother would not have allowed me to come on the voyage otherwise."

As she spoke she thought it sounded conceited and there was a flush on her cheeks as she said in a low voice:

"That is not quite . . . true because . . . actually I had no . . . alternative!"

"For which I am very grateful!" Ramón de Lopez replied conventionally. "Shall we start work?"

She knew that he was being tactful in helping her over an embarrassing moment and gratefully she waited for his first words of dictation.

The report was completed that day.

Therefore, Cañuela told herself, there would be no reason for her to be in Ramón de Lopez's Sitting-Room except to take him in the type-scripts as she finished typing them.

She wore her spectacles at meal-times, but now she had the feeling that he was looking through them, seeking her eyes as he had never done before.

He said nothing that could in any way be misconstrued but some instinct, because she was a woman, told her that he admired her.

It was impossible not to remember the expression on his face when he had walked into her cabin and seen her holding the sleeping child in her arms.

"Yet there is no comparison between me and Señora Sánchez!" Cañuela told herself.

But she knew, because of their work together, that there was a closeness between her and Ramón de Lopez which he had never had with any other woman.

He might make love to them; he might desire them; but she had stimulated his brain and she had been useful to him.

It only remained to see how long that usefulness would last.

Strangely, it seemed to her, he no longer tried to provoke her as he had done at the beginning of the voyage.

There seemed to be innumerable matters about which he wished to ask her advice but they all were impersonal and political. Yet Cañuela felt herself flattered because he listened to what she had to say.

Yet he was a man who had seen her defenceless, undressed with her hair over her shoulders!

A man!

When they first caught sight of the Coast of South

America far off in the West, Cañuela had a feeling of apprehension she had not expected.

"What lies ahead?" she asked herself. "Will the Señor find me of no further use to him?"

There must be in Buenos Aires dozens of people already employed by him to do the work that she had been doing.

Would he want her to return immediately to England?

They had never discussed the termination of her employment and she was very conscious of the fact that her return-ticket was in her hand-bag.

At any time he could thank her for what she had done and she would be on her way home.

What would she do when she reached London alone? How could she bear to stay in the Bed-Sitting Room in Bloomsbury without her mother?

For everyone else on board ship the end of the voyage meant the excitement of approaching home. There were signs of restlessness amongst the passengers.

The Officers looked smarter and the sailors were all busy polishing, painting, and scouring every possible part of the ship.

The vivid blue of the Atlantic began to give way to the muddy hue of the River Plate.

It was the Spaniards who had christened it The Rio de la Plata, meaning "The River of Silver," but it described nothing but a Spanish dream.

Its waters were muddied by the silt of vast plantations and the decaying vegetation of enormous forests. The River did not flow through "regions rich in mines of silver."

Cañuela was standing on deck, looking in the far distance towards the first sight of the domes, cupolas, and spires of Buenos Aires. Without turning her head she knew that Ramón de Lopez had joined her.

"Is it the end or the beginning of an adventure?" he asked.

"I suppose it is the . . . end," Cañuela replied.

She realised as she spoke that her voice sounded dull and despondent.

"That will be for you to decide," he answered. "We each make our own destiny."

"That is not true," Cañuela replied, thinking of her father.

"I think you will find you will make yours!"

She glanced at him wonderingly, not understanding what he was saying.

Looking away from her towards the city at the masts and shipping of all nations lining each side of the mouth of the River, he said:

"I really came to ask you what I should do with the boxes of orchids that are still stowed in the refrigerators."

There was a hint of amusement in his voice as if he realised that Cañuela had expected a more momentous or difficult question.

"I think if you were to give them to the Stewardesses to wear when they go ashore," she replied, "they would be delighted."

"I will do that," he answered, "and if you are interested I have thought of the flower you resemble."

"What is it?" Cañuela enquired.

"I do not suppose you have heard of it," he said, "it is known to the Argentines as *Lágrimas de la Virgen.*"

Before Cañuela could answer he had walked away.

She stood looking out at the River, remembering only too well exactly what the *Lágrimas de la Virgen* was like. The words meant "Tears of the Virgin."

It was a small lily with an exquisite fragrance which grew in tussocks like bushes, each plant composed of twenty or thirty stalks which were about two and a half feet high.

During the blooming season every stem produced a dozen or more flowers growing singly amongst the leaves, the shape and size of an English wild-rose.

But the strange thing about *Lágrimas de la Virgen* was that when the flowering stalks were picked the lovely and delicate petals would immediately drop off.

Its extreme frailty and sensitiveness made the

country-folk believe that it had a special spirituality about it so that no human being could make it theirs.

Then Cañuela remembered something else.

The *gauchos* in the South had a different name for the lily—they called it "The Tears of Love."

FIVE

Cañuela had packed all her own belongings, also the books and papers which concerned Ramón de Lopez, when she realised that she had left a box of pencils in his Sitting-Room.

She entered the cabin and, finding it empty, crossed to where she had left the pencils on a table opposite the chair on which she habitually sat to take dictation.

As she picked them up Ramón de Lopez came through the door which led to his bed-room.

He looked at Cañuela and realised that she was ready to go ashore.

Today she was wearing the elegant blue travelling-gown which belonged to her mother.

Because it was warm there was no need for her to cover it with the matching cape which was thickly lined, but instead she intended to put on at the last moment a short jacket which buttoned to the waist.

Her bonnet was more elaborate than anything she had worn in England. Like the dress, it had come from Paris and had that indefinable chic which somehow could never be emulated by other nations.

"You have packed everything, Miss Gray?" Ramón de Lopez asked.

"I hope so, Señor."

"There will be members of my staff to see to the heavy baggage," he informed her, "and there will be a carriage at the Quay waiting to carry you and me to my house."

He paused and added:

"I will tip your Stewardess."

"There is no need to do that, Señor," Cañuela replied. "She looked after me well, and I will give her what is necessary."

"I am sure you will need your money for other things."

"I still prefer to tip my own Stewardess."

It appeared that her words irritated him.

"Heavens above!" he exclaimed. "Must you argue over every little detail? The Stewards on this ship will be tipped by me, as they have always been."

He sounded so irritable that Cañuela said a little uncertainly:

"You have given me so much . . . already, and I have my . . . pride."

"Pride!" he exclaimed. "It was you, Miss Gray, who reminded me that pride goes before a fall, and one day that will happen to you."

Cañuela looked at him in surprise.

"What do you . . . mean?"

"I mean," he replied almost savagely, "that one day you will be humble; you will be gentle and tender, compassionate and in tears!"

Through her spectacles Cañuela stared at him in astonishment as he added:

"And when you cry you will know that you are in love!"

Cañuela drew in her breath.

"That, Señor," she said quietly, "is something that will never happen to me! But I will leave you to remunerate the Stewardess."

She walked from the cabin, closing the door behind her.

Only as she walked along the corridor did she realise that inexplicably she was trembling.

"Why do I irritate him so much?" she asked herself.

Why because she tried to behave in what she thought was the correct manner must he find it so annoying?

There was no answer to her questions and twenty minutes later she realised that the ship had docked, the gang-planks were in position, and she must go ashore.

Before the passengers could disembark a whole

crowd of friends and relations came surging onto the ship.

Cañuela remembered how in the old days there had always been a number of officials from the Legation and a host of her father and mother's friends waiting to greet them.

There had been flowers for her mother and usually boxes of chocolates for herself.

The scene had always seemed to be a dramatic homecoming and there were so many experiences to relate, so much gossip to hear.

It seemed strange that today there would be no-one even to speak to her.

She saw Señor Juan Sánchez, florid and red-faced, greet his wife and then look round at the crowd of passengers waiting to disembark, scrutinising each of them.

It seemed to Cañuela, although she might be imaginative, that when his eyes rested on Ramón de Lopez he frowned.

However, he walked across to him and held out his hand.

"How are you, de Lopez?" he enquired. "I heard you might be on board this ship."

"Glad to be home," Ramón de Lopez replied.

He turned towards the Señora, who had followed her husband, and raised his hat.

"I hope, Señora, you enjoyed the voyage?" he asked conventionally. "It is regrettable that we could see so little of each other, but unfortunately business occupied every moment of my time."

"Business?" Señor Sánchez asked suspiciously.

"You will hear all about it later," Ramón de Lopez promised. "It is a draft for the Government to peruse, and I think as Minister of Finance it will be of particular interest to you."

He turned away as he spoke, and with a gesture indicated to Cañuela that she should precede him down the gang-plank.

A great number of friends were waiting on the Quay, to greet Ramón de Lopez and exchange a few words with him on his arrival home.

Finally he managed to extricate himself and seated side by side with Cañuela in an elegant open carriage drawn by a pair of highly bred horses, they set off from the docks towards the center of the town.

To return to Buenos Aires was to Cañuela like stepping back into the past.

Every street seemed familiar and an indivisible part of her childhood.

Even the names of the different parts of Buenos Aires came back to her with a magical, musical ring which reminded her of fairy-tales.

Palermo with its infinity of gardens; La Recoleta with its ancient and shaded trees; El Pasque Lezama with its dells of mystery, and La Costanera with its beautiful promenade strung with high poplars.

It was all part of the magic of Buenos Aires which her father had fostered in her mind when he had told her stories of how Argentina came into being.

At first the Spaniards had neglected the town because at that time they were interested only in bullion, and the natural fauna except for the ostrich yielded nothing marketable abroad.

But standing on a great River coloured like a lion, the town was to grow and grow and with its growing become a mixture of English severity combined with the coloured patios of old Lima.

Ramón de Lopez drove for a little while in silence, and then as they reached a more important part of the city Cañuela gave an exclamation.

Here the streets and the houses were decked with bunting and flags.

Men were erecting banners which would cross the whole thoroughfare, others were draping lamp-posts and arranging arches which at night would be illuminated with gas-globes.

Cañuela suddenly remembered what day of the month it was and as she did so Ramón de Lopez said:

"Tomorrow is the twenty-fifth of May, Independence Day. You will see Buenos Aires at its gayest!"

"The decorations are very colourful," Cañuela replied.

She hoped that her voice sounded surprised and

knew she must not reveal that she was well aware how gay the city could be on Independence Day.

There would be banners and music, big processions and fire-works everywhere.

The *Te Deum* would be chanted in the Cathedral, which the President and his Ministers would attend dressed in all their regalia.

Then as she well knew the population would turn out *en masse,* thronging the streets, blocking the traffic, and hanging over the balconies so that they could watch the parades.

There would be a tremendous amount of noise, for when the Argentines rejoiced they always made a noise!

In every obscure village as well as in the Capital there would be fire-works from dawn to dusk, bombs and rockets bursting in the clouds with reports like thunder.

Also because it was Carnival there would be endless jokes which would sometimes become too rough to be amusing.

Lionel Arlington had often told Cañuela how unpleasant the Carnival could be when he first came to Argentina.

"If you dared to stir out of the house," he said, "it would be to expose yourself as a target for hundreds of unseen pelters."

"What do the pelters throw?" Cañuela had asked.

"Pomitos," he replied, "packets of finely chipped paper filled with flour or small pebbles. You can imagine what a temptation they were to small boys."

Cañuela had laughed.

"And if one did not receive *pomitos* in the face or over one's clothes," her father continued, "there was a considerable risk of getting a drenching with water, being covered with flour, or pelted with eggs and even stones."

"It sounds horrible!" Cañuela exclaimed.

"It became so rough," her father answered, "that water throwing in the cities was prohibited by the Police, and the *pomitos* are supposed to contain nothing more offensive than scent!"

The Carnival Cañuela had seen three years ago had been a very colourful affair.

She had watched it from a balcony at the British Legation and been delighted with the processions carrying Holy images.

There had been groups of young men belonging to Clubs or organisations dressed either as "mummers" or in historical costumes.

It had all seemed very good-humoured and the *gauchos* riding in the races which were very much a part of Independence Day were in Cañuela's mind the most thrilling of them all.

Many of them saved the whole year for an entirely new rig-out.

The trappings of their horses were cleaned and polished, manes and tails close-cropped, and they vied with each other in seeing who could display the greatest amount of silver, not only on their mounts but on themselves.

Proud as the Knights of Medieval times, they rode forth to test their equestrian skill against all on-comers.

The races themselves were simply a test of the intrepidity of the rider and the speed and endurance of the animal. But both were tried to the utmost of their powers.

The prizes and trophies were greatly valued as momentos of outstanding horsemanship.

"You will be able to watch the processions tomorrow from my house," Ramón de Lopez was saying. "I expect when I arrive home I shall find a great many other things have been arranged in my absence in which I must take part."

He did not say more and Cañuela felt as if he was warning her about something.

It was not a long drive to the Plaza Victoria, the principle square.

She saw again the Cathedral which sheltered the burial place of St. Martin, the Archbishop's Palace, and the Casa Rosa, pink and splendid, the home of the President.

Then they were in the Plaza St. Martin and she

saw a number of what her mother had described as "the Palaces" of the aristocracy.

Surrounded by their gardens and gleaming white they were very impressive in the warm sunshine.

Ramón de Lopez's house was all that Cañuela might have expected of it and more.

To begin with it was enormous, and when she entered it she found that a cool dimness protected it from the glare of the burning sun.

The atmosphere had nothing to do with pomp and splendour or even luxury.

She could not explain it to herself except that the house seemed welcoming.

Then she told herself that it was just an illusion because it reminded her of the years of happiness she had spent in Buenos Aires.

Her mother had spoken of Ramón de Lopez as having an "army of servants" and there certainly seemed an inordinate number of them.

Finally one whom Cañuela gathered was the Housekeeper took her upstairs to her room.

As was usual in Argentina the house was built round several court-yards but never could Cañuela remember seeing anything as beautiful as a big, carved stone fountain which was throwing its water iridescent into the sun.

It was surrounded by a profusion of flowers, so exquisite they were a poem of colour.

There were orange trees bearing their fruit and creepers like hybiscus and bougainvillaea vivid against white marble.

It was all so lovely that Cañuela felt speechless, and when she was shown into her bed-room she realised that it too was a complementary part of "the Palace."

"I hope you will be comfortable, Señorita," the Housekeeper said. "I have allotted a maid to look after you. Her name is Dolores."

"Thank you," Cañuela said.

A moment later Dolores entered the room.

She was very attractive; with an oval face and large, dark, lustrous eyes fringed with long lashes. Cañuela guessed that she was about seventeen.

Dolores curtsied and said how honoured she was to serve the gracious lady from overseas.

The luggage was brought upstairs and as Dolores unpacked she chatted away in a friendly fashion which was so much a part of the Argentine character.

"Are you looking forward to tomorrow?" Cañuela asked, knowing what an important day it was for the citizens of Buenos Aires.

"I have a new dress, Señorita, with which to go dancing with my fiancé. My father and mother will of course accompany us," she added quickly in case Cañuela should think there was anything wrong in such behaviour.

"Of course," Cañuela agreed.

She was well aware that Argentine girls were forever under the eye of their parents or a *duenna*.

"Girls of all classes are never out of leading-strings," she had heard her father say once, "from the cradle to the marriage-bed, so that their virtue is exposed to no temptations."

It was rather the same, Cañuela thought, as the way English girls were chaperoned and never for a moment allowed to be alone with a man.

She was well aware how exceptional it had been for her to spend, as she had done after Madeira, twelve days, to all intents and purposes, alone with Ramón de Lopez.

She thought of how shocked her mother's contemporaries of the past would have been, and indeed her father would never have allowed it.

She was not afraid that if she met any of his friends in Buenos Aires they would recognise her.

As a school-girl she had never been allowed to attend any functions because she had not yet made her début.

She ate her meals in the School-Room with her Governess.

She went for walks in the Park and round the town with Miss Johnson and there was no question of her going to the races.

A visit to the theatre was permitted to see a special

performance of Shakespeare or one of the classical authors, but only to a matinée.

'I have been more free since I started work,' Cañuela thought to herself, 'than any other girl of my age and position is ever likely to be.'

Then she knew that that was the right expression —a "girl in her position."

She was a girl who could play no part in Society because her father had been considered a traitor.

She was a girl whom no decent person in Buenos Aires would wish to know, had they any idea of her identity.

She felt herself tremble in case she should be found out, and wondered what Ramón de Lopez's reaction would be if she was.

He had obviously believed her father to be guilty. Would he therefore send her back to England without even a word of gratitude for all she had done for him?

She could not believe he would do that, and yet how could she trust anyone?

Had Ramón de Lopez not turned against her father, who had believed him to be a friend?

Had he not like all the other Argentines been only too willing to defame and destroy a man whom he had praised and exalted for years?

"No-one must ever find me out," Cañuela said to herself.

When the time came for her to leave she would slip away unnoticed and return to obscurity.

She even thought that she and her mother might change their name once again.

Having changed it once, what did it matter if they did so dozens of times?

If only she could make enough money, she and her mother could move from place to place, unobtrusive, unnoticed. Two shadows with whom no-one need concern themselves.

Cañuela gave a little sigh and pressed her spectacles even further on her small nose.

They secured her anonymity from prying eyes. They were her shield.

"I must be careful, very careful," she warned herself, "not to reveal that I have ever been here before."

A little later in the day she was shown a small office next to a huge room where, she learnt, Ramón de Lopez sat when he was working.

A member of his secretarial staff informed Cañuela of her duties.

"The Señor has asked that you will deal with all matters appertaining to England, and the report, which I understand the Señor dictated while you were on board ship."

Cañuela inclined her head.

"Cablegrams and letters from England will be brought to you, Señorita, unopened on their arrival," the man went on. "If there is anything you want, please be kind enough to ask for me. My name is Náon—Marcela Náon."

"Thank you, Señor Náon," Cañuela said. "I will try not to worry you more than is necessary, but you understand I may find some things strange and difficult to understand."

"I shall be only too pleased and delighted to be of assistance, Señorita," was the reply.

It was delightful to get back to the courtesy and sometimes long-winded politeness of Argentina.

There was none of the sharp, authoritative manner of speaking which Cañuela had found in the office in London.

Here everyone was courteous and respectful, if sometimes a little flamboyant.

But it had an old-world charm and was far more pleasant to listen to than the curtness that had sometimes made her wince.

At the same time Cañuela knew too well that such a pleasant manner of speaking often reflected the inefficiency which lay behind most business relations in the Argentine.

"You can sum it all up in a few words," her father had said laughingly. *"Mañana, pasado mañana, la semana que viene."*

"Tomorrow, the day after tomorrow, next week," Cañuela had translated.

They were her safe-guard.

"Exactly!" he said. "Everything will be settled in time. In the meantime it will tax their utmost ingenuity to defer the settlement indefinitely!"

That evening Cañuela dined alone.

She learnt from the servants that Señor Lopez was dining out.

Her own meal had been arranged in a small Dining-Room where she gathered the Señor breakfasted and which looked out onto the court-yard.

She found by this time that the house extended almost indefinitely.

There were other court-yards and far at the back, reaching out into the garden, a huge Ball-Room.

The garden itself was very beautiful, shaded by acacia trees and filled with all the brilliant and beautiful flowers she had missed when in England.

She wondered if she would ever have time to sit out in the sunshine and dream as she had dreamt when she was young.

She had believed then that the world was filled with noble, kind, friendly people whom she would love and who would love her.

Everything that lay ahead of her had seemed as golden and wonderful as the *Pampas*. The poet's "treeless plain" an immense open country which under a driving wind looked "like a high sea flowing."

It stirred her imagination and made her feel that it was like her life stretching out towards a limitless horizon.

She was to learn all too bitterly that her horizon, limited by treachery and lack of money, was to become one small Bed-Sitting Room in Bloomsbury.

Yet for the moment she had escaped!

"I must enjoy this. I must remember it. I must impress it on my mind," Cañuela told herself, "so that I can never forget."

She thought that when Señor Lopez had no further use for her and she was back in England again she would be able to shut her eyes and see the colours that enchanted her.

She would hear too the song of the birds which had been a music she would never forget.

Sometimes when London had been very dark and grey, foggy or pouring with rain, she had been able to visualise the flowing, shallow marshy rivers of the *Pampas* to which her father had taken her on their rides.

Avoiding patches of giant thistles, they had ridden to lower ground where the grass was almost waist-high and full of flowers.

It had been like an English meadow in June and they had found the streams which at times would swell with the rains to become wide rivers.

And there would be an astonishing number of birds. Wild duck, swans, waders, ibises, herons, spoonbills, all of which her father would point out.

And sometimes, most exciting of all, Cañuela would see tall white-and-rose-coloured birds which when they opened their wings revealed a glorious crimson colour.

They were flamingos, but although she continually looked for them she only saw them on special occasions.

"I must remember. I must remember everything!" she told herself now.

It had been hard to tear herself away from the garden and return to the cool, quiet of the house.

She finished her dinner and walked out into the court-yard.

The stone fountain was a very old Spanish one which had been exquisitely carved by craftsmen long since dead.

She was aware of the complicated filigree stone engravings that were the achievement of Indian craftsmen who had been employed by the Jesuits.

The soft patter of the water falling into a stone basin prevented her from hearing anyone approach.

She jumped when quite unexpectedly she heard Ramón de Lopez's voice ask:

"Are you admiring my fountain, Miss Gray?"

"It is beautiful!" Cañuela said spontaneously. "But then the Indian carvings are always . . ."

She realised suddenly that what she was about to say

would make her seem too knowledgeable about them and continued quickly:

". . . are always described in books as being outstandingly lovely."

"That is true," he said. "Have you explored the rest of my house?"

"I have seen some of it," Cañuela answered.

"And the garden?"

"The garden is very beautiful."

It was almost, she felt, as if he was forcing her to admire his possessions and then he said:

"Tomorrow, on Independence Day, it is usual for everyone to give a party. It was arranged before I left that there would be a Ball for my friends in this house, which we would share with the one next door, which is owned by a member of the Government."

He paused. Cañuela said nothing, wondering why he was bothering to explain this to her.

"At Carnival-time it is amusing to be anonymous," Ramón de Lopez said, "and all my guests and those of my joint host will wear masks. The majority will also be in fancy-dress. I hope you will accept my invitation to be present."

For a moment Cañuela was still thinking that she had not understood him and then she said:

"As a guest?"

"As a guest!" Ramón de Lopez repeated. "I am not commanding you to appear, Miss Gray, but inviting you to do so."

Cañuela had an impulse to say yes, but then she realised only too well what it would entail.

There would be people there whom she might have met before. If there were, she could have nothing to say to them, and to everyone else she would be a stranger.

It was not likely that Ramón de Lopez as a host would have much time to speak to her.

She would know nobody.

She would wander round feeling shy and embarrassed and afraid every moment, even though it was impossible that someone might guess she was the daughter of Lionel Arlington.

"It is very gracious of you to ask me, Señor," she said, "but I must refuse your invitation."

"Why?" he asked abruptly.

"Because I have no wish to go to a party."

"That is an absurd excuse, as you know," he replied. "You are young and all young people want to dance, especially at Carnival-time."

"You are speaking of Argentines, Señor. I am English."

"You are still young. Even the English dance!"

He smiled.

"As you well know, while I was in London I was invited to a Ball every night, on some evenings two or three Balls."

"It is hardly the same thing in my case, Señor."

"English hostesses welcomed me with open arms. As an Argentine host I am prepared to do the same thing where you are concerned."

"I thank you, but I have given you my answer."

"Are you being difficult once again?"

"Not difficult, but practical," Cañuela answered. "I am your employee and you know as well as I do that the guests who will come to your Ball tomorrow night would not expect to rub shoulders with a mere secretary, and they would be extremely affronted were they to be inadvertently introduced to one."

Ramón de Lopez did not speak for a moment, but Cañuela knew that what she had said was irrefutable.

Society in Argentina was straitlaced and extremely narrow in some aspects.

Argentines rather like the English, believed that the structure of Society rested on the preservation of respectability.

What was more, Argentines of all classes believed in the ideal of purity, incorruptibility, and honourable conduct.

This was all based on a social code which as far as a family was concerned was both narrow and bigotted.

It would have been impossible, Cañuela knew, even for Mrs. Arlington, with all her kindness, understanding, and sympathy, to have invited one of her husband's secretaries to luncheon to meet her women-friends.

It would have been just as impossible for any Argentine hostess to acknowledge or even meet Cañuela, as she was Ramón de Lopez's secretary and had travelled unchaperoned with him from Southampton to Buenos Aires.

"Everyone will be masked," Ramón de Lopez said in a low voice. "I would like you to be present."

"To do what? To see what? To hear what?" Cañuela enquired.

He did not reply and she said:

"I am very conscious of my position, Señor. I belong to your office and there I must remain."

He gave a little sigh.

"I thought perhaps you were more adventurous and less stereotyped than most English girls of your age."

She did not answer and he said, as if explaining things to himself:

"But then the average English girl would certainly not have your intelligence or, surprisingly, your education!"

"An English girl, if she was the type of person you would invite to your Ball, would not be working for you, Señor. It is therefore quite obvious that I should keep my place."

"I am just wondering what that is," he said reflectively.

"I have been informed that it is to deal with your English correspondence. I dare say there will be a number of cablegrams tomorrow morning. If you will be at the Carnival I will not trouble you with them until the following day."

"You are most considerate, Miss Gray!"

There was a note of sarcasm in his voice.

"I try to be, Señor."

She dropped him a small curtsy and turned away.

She knew without looking round that he was watching her go.

She hoped that she was walking with dignity and even grace.

Then she told herself sharply that she had no right to think such things.

What did it matter how she walked?

She was a secretary and nothing more and she should not even take it as a compliment that he had invited her to his party.

It had been, she told herself, a desire to show off.

He wanted her to see him surrounded by the élite of Buenos Aires; to admire the way his Ball would be organised; to see the beauty of his garden lit with gas-globes and flickering candles.

"Fairy-lights" she had called them when she was a child, and she remembered leaning over the balcony and watching her father and mother dancing on the lawn while the fairy-lights flickered amongst the trees and flowers.

There had been Chinese lanterns to cast a golden glow over small arbours where couples could sit out and talk to each other when they were not dancing.

Her mother had looked like a fairy-Princess.

Cañuela pictured her in the white gown which now lay in her trunk because her mother had insisted she bring it with her.

"Poor Mama—she has no idea what sort of position I hold," Cañuela told herself.

As far as she was concerned there would be no white gowns, no dancing amongst the fairy-lights; no taking part in the Carnival on Independence Day, when all Argentina went mad.

Despite the fact that Cañuela slept on the inside court-yard, she was awakened soon after dawn by the rockets screeching into the sky.

As she dressed the noise grew louder and louder, and soon there were the drums and trumpets of the Bands to be heard in the far distance and the ringing of Church-bells.

Every hour or so there was also the stirring strains of the National Anthem, which Lionel Arlington had once described as a "musical, patriotic, and poetic masterpiece."

The servants were bustling busily about the house in a fashion which Cañuela knew was unusual.

When she reached her office she found that there were no cables and no letters.

She realised that she had forgotten, when she had spoken to Ramón de Lopez the night before, that the postal-services would undoubtedly come to a full stop on the gayest and most irresponsible day of the year!

It was therefore inevitable that she should find herself sooner or later standing with Señor Náon on the balcony together with several other senior members of the staff.

There was a procession passing down the street, carrying an enormous carved image of a Saint and innumerable embroidered banners from the Churches.

There were penitents wearing monks' robes, walking bare-footed and telling Rosaries, following the Sacred Image.

There were soldiers helping to push other Holy relics down the cobbled road and it seemed to Cañuela as if a thousand brazen trumpets filled the air.

People were cheering, laughing, and singing, and there was an irrepressible gaiety everywhere.

Small boys were of course throwing *pomitos,* many of which, Cañuela was certain, did not contain only harmless scent.

From the balconies women threw flowers to the marching soldiers and the *gauchos.*

They would be deftly caught, placed in the cap, behind an ear or thrust into the front of a buttoned tunic with a smile which was received with a languorous glance.

Cañuela knew that the flowers of the Carnival meant the start of hundreds of new *affaires de coeur.*

Some would end in marriage later in the year, many would end in tears.

Respectable women did not venture onto the streets, but for the men there were a profusion of lovely, provocative faces with inviting lips and flashing eyes.

"Perhaps tonight instead of going to the Ball I could go into the street!" Cañuela told herself.

Then she thought of how horrified her mother would have been at such an idea!

The day passed quickly with so much to watch, so much to see.

In the afternoon Cañuela knew that everyone of importance had gone to the races.

It was her one regret that she had been too young to attend them when she was here before.

Now there was no chance of her being in the special enclosure which was reserved for the aristocracy of Buenos Aires.

She did not mind about that, but she would have liked to see the horses, and she would have enjoyed the races.

But most of all she would have liked to see the gaiety and enthusiasm of the crowds.

Her father had described it all to her so often. How to win a race was to sweep those who had backed the winner into Heaven itself! How to lose was to produce a despondency which often made the emotional people shed tears of frustration.

Ramón de Lopez would of course be running his horses, which were noted as being the best in the whole of Argentina.

Because he was such a popular figure, more people would put their money on him for his individual qualities than for the excellence of his stable.

And when he won, as undoubtedly he would, because he spent more money than anyone else on his bloodstock, it would increase his popularity and carry him one day further forward towards the time when he would become President.

It seemed strange that Argentina should be celebrating so wildly eighty-four years later the Independence that they gained on May 25, 1810.

After that date no representative of Spanish power ever again exercised authority in Buenos Aires, nor in any but a corner of the Viceroyalty of the Rio de la Plata, and not there for long.

On the day Independence was born, the Spanish

Viceroy, the Marquis de Sobremonte, fled from his Capital city.

As Lionel Arlington often told Cañuela, there were men loyal to Spain who were to play leading parts in the future events but initiative in political organisation and in political action had passed to the Creole community.

When the Viceroy fled from Buenos Aires and allowed it to pass without serious resistance into hostile hands, he sent orders to Montevideo to despatch troops to the interior.

But he had lost control. The people struck out for themselves to liberate their cities, the Pampas, and the great River which flowed through them.

There was a great deal of fighting; a great deal of suffering; but finally Argentina as a nation came into being.

From that beginning, Cañuela thought, had grown up great families like that of Ramón de Lopez.

They retained all that was best in the Spanish character, discarded the worst, and became identified with the country until they had a personality that was all their own.

There was something about Ramón de Lopez, she thought, which was different from the men of other nations she had met.

She could not explain it even to herself, except that it was in part the pride, the self-sufficiency, and the arrogance that she had hated.

But she had grown to realise that it was intrinsically a faith in himself, and a belief in his own destiny.

He knew he could help Argentina. He knew that he had a solution for many of the problems which were oppressing the economy and the people at this particular moment.

Cañuela could not help thinking that if everyone believed in themselves so wholeheartedly much more would be accomplished.

Then she told herself that her father had believed in himself.

It was impossible not to feel a surge of hatred against

Argentina and all it contained! Yet, at the same time, she loved even while she hated.

The household became increasingly busy, making arrangements for the evening.

Cañuela walked into the garden and saw the fairy-lights were all arranged, and large lanterns hung from the trees.

The windows of the Ball-Room had been removed so that the whole of one side of the huge room was open onto the garden.

It was a very beautiful room hung with great gilt mirrors and crystal chandeliers; the walls were papered with Chinese silk—patterned with flowers and exotic birds.

The floor was polished until she could almost see her face in it and she suddenly longed to dance as she had not been able to do for the last two years.

She had never been to a real Ball, but there had been parties given for the girls of her own age and often her father would dance with her in the evenings while her mother played the piano.

"You must dance well," he had said to Cañuela. "I cannot bear women who stumble and are not light in one's arms."

He smiled and added:

"Your mother is like thistledown. I have never met anyone so light or so graceful!"

"It is because I love dancing with you," her mother had laughed.

They had exchanged a glance of sheer happiness and, half-jealous because she was losing her father's attention, Cañuela had cried:

"Dance with me again, Papa! Please dance with me again!"

They had swept round the room in a waltz and then he had taught her how to tango, using exaggerated steps which had made her mother exclaim in horror:

"If Cañuela dances like that in a Ball-Room, the Dowagers would hold up their hands in horror!"

"And quite rightly!" her father had replied. "It is a very provocative dance."

"Provocative of what?" Cañuela had asked.

"I will tell you when you are older," her father answered.

Now moving through the garden, Cañuela found herself wondering how Ramón de Lopez would dance.

She was certain that it would be well.

Large though he was, he had the lithe strength of an Argentine who looked his best on horseback, but could also move with an inner grace over a Ball-Room floor.

The English, stiff, correct, and very conscious of their importance, never let themselves go in a manner that was essential if one was to be a good dancer.

"Yes, Ramón de Lopez would dance well," Cañuela sighed as she went upstairs.

She wondered if he would hold Señora Sánchez in his arms, or if she would be too cautious to dance with him when her husband was present.

Whether Señora Sánchez would oblige him or not, there would be others, Cañuela thought, who would be only too eager.

A little later Dolores was to tell her so.

"It will be a very grand Ball tonight, Señorita," she said. "It is a pity we cannot watch, but the Señor has forbidden it."

Cañuela could understand that Ramón de Lopez did not wish the prying eyes of servants watching him and his guests.

"All the most beautiful women in Buenos Aires will come to the Señor's party," Dolores said with pride in her voice.

"There will be other parties," Cañuela remarked.

"Hundreds of them, Señorita, but there is only one Señor de Lopez, and the young ladies all want to marry him, while the others—how shall I put it—they want to be his—flirt!"

She spoke in Spanish and the word was not translatable, but the meaning was very clear.

"They find him . . . attractive?" Cañuela said almost as if speaking to herself.

"And who would not?" Dolores asked. "Everyone says the Señor is the most attractive, most alluring, and most passionate man in Buenos Aires!"

Cañuela did not know why but she felt as if something strange happened inside her.

"Passionate?" she questioned.

"But of course, Señorita, it is a compliment! It is what a man should be, and the Señor is noted for his many, many love-affairs!"

"Dolores," Cañuela said in a cold voice, "I would like you to bring my supper upstairs. It will save me leaving my room."

"I will do that, Señorita, but what a pity you cannot go to the Ball."

Cañuela had taken off her glasses and was sitting in a chair while Dolores laid out the dress she had exptected her to wear for supper.

"I am a secretary, Dolores," she said.

"I know that, Señorita, but you are beautiful . . . very beautiful! More beautiful than the ladies who will come to the Ball and pout their lips at the Señor, hoping that he will kiss them!"

"Surely not?" Cañuela protested. "It would not be at all the correct thing to do!"

Dolores laughed.

"Ah, Señorita, you do not know what goes on. We servants, we see many things! Married women who make an excuse to ask the Señor if he will advise them about a horse they wish to buy for their husband's birthday."

She laughed.

"Other ladies," she continued, "who contrive to lure him away from the lights when there is a Ball with the excuse that they feel faint, must sit down, or their slipper has come undone."

She made an expressive gesture.

"Ah—we have heard all the excuses and laugh about them!"

"And the Señor . . . accepts . . . such favours?" Cañuela asked.

"What man would refuse a delicious peach when he does not even have the trouble of picking it!"

Cañuela laughed.

At the same time she knew that there must be a great deal of truth in what Dolores was saying.

Women as beautiful as Señora Sánchez would want not only the company of Ramón de Lopez but the touch of his lips.

He was handsome, he was clever, he was rich!

He had a personality which made other men pale into insignificance beside him, and what was more, he was a bachelor!

"Why is the Señor not married?" she asked Dolores.

She knew it was incorrect for her to gossip with the servants.

At the same time she was so curious and there was no-one else with whom she could talk.

"Perhaps the Señor has never found a woman he really loves," Dolores replied. "All men are the same, they seek someone perfect, a woman they think is different! Whilst they themselves are neither!"

Again Cañuela laughed.

"You are very perceptive, Dolores. Who taught you to think such things?"

"My fiancé says I think too much and that I am too critical," Dolores answered, "but my father has always encouraged me."

"What does your father do?"

"He has a small pharmacy, Señorita, but he is very much liked and people come to buy from him because he amuses them! Sometimes he talks much more than he sells!"

"But you like being here, working in this house rather than in your father's shop?"

"I have to make money, Señorita. I want to get married so I save and save."

"That reminds me," Cañuela said, "I thought you were going out with your fiancé this evening. You told me you had bought a special dress for the occasion."

Dolores gave a little sigh.

"It was all planned," she said, "and then my fiancé's boss he offered much extra money to work tonight in the Restaurant and not to go to the Carnival. As I said, Señorita, we are both saving."

"Oh, Dolores, how disappointing!" Cañuela exclaimed.

"It is a great disappointment," Dolores agreed. "At

the same time, we can get married sooner. That is worth more than a dance at the Carnival!"

"You are very sensible!" Cañuela smiled.

"It is a waste of my pretty dress," Dolores said with a sigh, "but I will wear it next year."

"I hope so," Cañuela said.

Suddenly Dolores took a step towards her and said:

"I have an idea, Señorita. Why do you not wear my dress and go to the Ball?"

Cañuela looked at her in surprise.

"I can get you a mask," Dolores went on. "There are a great number of them downstairs in the Hall for the guests who arrive without them. No-one will go into the Ball-Room or the garden without being masked. If, Señorita, you wear my dress and cover your hair, no-one will know who you are."

"No . . . no!" Cañuela said. "It is very kind of you, Dolores, but it is impossible."

"But why?" Dolores persisted. "It could be an adventure. You are English. You have never seen a Ball in Buenos Aires. It is very grand! Last year I helped wait in the Ball-Room and never have I seen anything so exciting!"

She threw out her hands.

"There were hundreds of different costumes, each looking like a picture. Clowns and Columbines, Spanish warriors, ladies with huge white wigs, men dressed as devils, and lots, yes lots, Señorita, of ladies of quality wearing Spanish peasant-costumes."

Cañuela was listening, fascinated.

It was an absurd, ridiculous idea, and yet she could see that it was possible.

Dressed in the peasant-costume which Dolores had bought new for the occasion, with a handkerchief over her hair under a big sombrero, and masked, it would be doubtful if even her mother would recognize her.

She knew exactly the type of costume she would be wearing, for she had as a child worn one to a fancy-dress party.

Supposing . . . just supposing she should attend the Ball for just half an hour?

She could move round amongst the guests and see

the beautiful women who were trying to attract Ramón de Lopez.

She would watch them and perhaps once again she would spot a spy or a detective working on behalf of some jealous husband.

No . . . no . . . it was a ridiculous idea, and Dolores should not have suggested it to her!

"Wait a minute, Señorita," Dolores said, and went from the room.

Cañuela rose from the chair and walked towards the dressing-table.

She looked at herself in the mirror. In the light of the gas-globes with which the room was illuminated her hair gleamed more red than gold and her grey-green eyes were dark pools of mystery.

She remembered the expression in Ramón de Lopez's eyes when with the sleeping baby in her arms she had turned her face towards him as he stood inside her cabin.

He had been astonished—surprised!

At the same time there had been something else in his eyes; something she had seen in other men's.

"Who will he look at in that way tonight?" she asked herself.

Cañuela had the feeling that he was no longer interested in Señora Sánchez.

Their love-affair, if that was what it had been, had come to an abrupt end and he had been content to leave it that way.

But there would be other women.

The beautiful, alluring, exotic women of Buenos Aires, who like birds of Paradise would flaunt their dark hair and alabaster skins before him.

Cañuela could remember their full red lips and the sensuous movements of their bodies which she had once read were the symbols of a passionate and voluptuous nature.

Is that what Señor Ramón de Lopez wanted of his women?

She knew too that they had a grace and vivacity which the Señor would not have found in English ladies.

"They shock the eye and captivate the senses," an

impressionable young Diplomat had once told her father when she was listening.

"They are fine animals," Lionel Arlington had replied.

Then her mother had interposed:

"That is rude, Lionel! They are bewitching, delightful, and very lovely!"

Lionel Arlington had laughed.

"The acme of their ambition," he said, "is three things: to play the piano, to speak French, and to have a string of lovers!"

"Nonsense!" Mrs. Arlington had exclaimed, but she had laughed.

"There is only one thing wrong with Argentine women," her father had remarked more seriously, "apart from the fact that they do not appeal as you do to the soul."

"And what is that?" her mother enquired.

"Their voices!"

That, Cañuela knew, was true.

Argentine women often had voices that were harsh and slightly shrill.

It was surprising that with all their beauty, their voices were not more musical. She wondered if Ramón de Lopez had ever noticed it.

The door opened and Dolores came back into the room.

Over her arm she carried the red skirt, white embroidered blouse, and black velvet bodice of an Argentine peasant.

There were also the full, crisply laundered and starched white petticoats, the apron with its lace edging, and the silk handkerchief which was worn to conceal the hair under a big white sombrero.

"Is that your dress?" Cañuela asked unnecessarily.

"Now it is yours!" Dolores replied. "Put it on, Señorita, I want to see how lovely you look in it!"

SIX

"You look very beautiful, Señorita," Dolores exclaimed.

Cañuela's reflection in the mirror told her that the costume was in fact very becoming.

The tight black bodice revealed the slimness of her waist and the low-cut muslin blouse embroidered with red smocking enhanced the white transparency of her skin.

The red handkerchief concealed her hair under the wide sombrero and her eyes looked enormous in her tiny face.

"Put on the mask, Señorita," Dolores suggested.

She had collected one from downstairs while Cañuela was dressing and now she held it out. Cañuela saw that it was a dainty affair, but nevertheless very concealing.

The part that went over the nose and round the eyes was of velvet, but attached to the bottom of it, Venetian fashion, was a frill of black lace which almost completely hid the lips.

She put it on and realised that it would be a very perceptive person indeed who would guess her identity.

"Now you must go to the Ball," Dolores declared.

"I cannot . . . you know I cannot!" Cañuela protested.

"But why not, Señorita?" Dolores enquired. "I promise you, no-one will recognise you, and you'll be thrilled as I was with all the wonderful costumes."

She lowered her voice as if someone might overhear and added:

"I'll tell you a secret: the Señor is dressed in the costume of an English aristocrat of many years ago."

"I wonder if it will be sufficient disguise?" Cañuela said more to herself than to Dolores.

Then she thought that what she ought to do was take off Dolores's clothes immediately and go to bed.

It was unthinkable in her position that she should join the merry-makers downstairs, and yet Ramón de Lopez had invited her to come as his guest.

She had suspected his motives.

At the same time she could not excuse her timidity by claiming that she had not been invited.

Was it timidity, shyness, or cowardice?

Cañuela asked herself the question and felt ashamed.

She had never been a coward.

She had always thought of herself as brave and adventurous, and yet for some unknown reason she was afraid to embark on what, after all, would be a small adventure.

She was only to be a spectator—a looker-on at some festivities which were important only to the Argentines themselves.

Supposing she went for just a few minutes—just to see the gardens, the lights, and the decorated Ball-Room?

As if she sensed that her hesitation was a prelude to capitulation, Dolores said:

"Come, Señorita—come quickly! The only danger of being recognised is if you are seen walking down the stairs. But I'll take you a different way and once you are in the Ball-Room you'll be lost in the crowd."

That was true, Cañuela thought five minutes later!

She was lost in the crowd.

No-one, she was sure, would notice her as she moved amongst the gaily dressed people walking round the gardens, dancing in the Ball-Room, or standing in groups talking to one another.

There appeared to be quite a number of women like herself, alone, or perhaps searching for one particular man amongst so many unidentifiable males.

Dolores had been right in saying that the costumes were entrancing.

There were innumerable Columbines, Ballet Dancers, Harlequins, and clowns.

There were a number of crinolines and huge eighteenth-century wigs in the mode affected by Marie-Antoinette.

There were half a dozen "Portias" in red silk, a costume particularly becoming to dark hair, and an equal number of "Persephones," who were wearing, Cañuela was sure, blonde wigs.

Then, because she had been looking for him, although she would not admit it to herself, she saw Ramón de Lopez.

He came from the Ball-Room into the garden, escorting a very dramatically attired "Carmen."

He was wearing the close-fitting, long-tailed evening-coat and the tight champagne-coloured pantaloons of a Georgian gentleman. His crisp, white muslin cravat was high against the sharp line of his chin.

He was masked, but Cañuela felt that she would have recognised him anywhere.

It was impossible not to remember the squareness of his forehead, which she had looked at across the table in the Dining-Saloon of the ship for twelve days; or the thick darkness of his hair and the curve of his lips.

She remembered how they could twist in a cynical smile or be set in a hard line when she incensed him.

He was talking animatedly to his companion, and hastily Cañuela moved in the opposite direction.

Then she realised that they were walking towards the flower-beds where there was only the beguiling glow of the lanterns and the twinkling fairy-lights leading deeper into the darkness of the trees.

Cañuela could not help wondering what excuse the alluring "Carmen" by Ramón de Lopez's side had used to entice him to such a secluded spot.

Then she told herself that he would not need an excuse.

He had led, as she well knew, an austere, monk-like existence aboard the ship, and he would be seeking again the charms and favours of seductive women.

With an effort Cañuela told herself that this was not the moment to dwell on what Ramón de Lopez might be doing in the garden, but to seize her opportunity to see the Ball-Room.

She went in through one of the large openings from which the windows had been removed.

She had not realised when she had visited the room earlier in the day that Ramón de Lopez had intended it to be lit only by candles.

They cast a soft alluring light on the women waltzing with their partners on the polished floor.

There were flowers everywhere—in garlands draped along the walls, banked in each corner, and almost obscuring the Band playing on a small platform.

There was the fragrance of flowers, the scent of exotic perfumes, and the chatter of voices which seemed to mingle with the sentimental melody of the music.

It was all very lovely, at the same time exciting for someone who had never been to a grown-up Ball.

Cañuela saw for the first time how elegant a woman could look when she danced, her full skirt swirling round her like the petals of a flower, her head thrown back to look up at her partner's face.

The waltz came to an end and now the dancers were moving into the garden or towards the long buffets in the big Ante-Room opening out of the Ball-Room.

Cañuela was just wondering if she was conspicuous standing alone when the music started up again. This time it was a tango.

She had always wanted to see it danced as her father had taught it to her, so now it was impossible for her to go and she could only stand watching the grace with which the intricate and sometimes difficult steps were being enacted in front of her.

It was then that she heard a voice which she recognised say to her in Spanish:

"May I, Señorita, have the pleasure of this dance?"

Her heart gave a frightened leap and even before she turned her head she knew who stood there.

For a moment she was incapable of speaking.

She felt as if her voice had died in her throat.

Then as if he took her acceptance for granted Ramón de Lopez put his arm round her waist and drew her onto the floor.

She could feel the firmness of his hand on her waist. Because it would have been out of character to wear gloves with her peasant's-costume her own hands were bare.

She found that Ramón de Lopez's left hand was also gloveless, and as he touched her fingers she felt a strange quiver run through her which she thought must be fear.

'I am afraid I will not dance well enough for him,' she thought.

But she realised that they were moving almost perfectly in unison and in some strange manner she was aware of what he was about to do even as he did it.

It might have been the pressure of his hand on her waist or the fact that she was so close to him, she did not know.

She knew only that it was completely and utterly effortless to follow whatever step he wished to perform, and there was nothing for her to think about except the joy of dancing with a man who was obviously an expert.

They had moved halfway round the room before he spoke again.

"You are enjoying the Ball?"

Cañuela was about to reply when she realised that if she answered him in Spanish he might recognise her voice.

She hesitated momentarily.

As she did so an idea came to her.

"It is a very delightful occasion, *Signor,*" she answered in Italian.

Ramón de Lopez had never heard her speak Italian, and although she was not as proficient in the language as she was in Spanish or Portuguese she had learnt Italian from Maria, who had been first her Nurse and then her maid.

Lionel Arlington had insisted that she should also have Italian lessons but Cañuela had learnt from Maria the underworld Italian called "Lunfardo."

It was an argot evolved by the Italian immigrants and used in most Argentine songs, especially the tango.

Whatever else Ramón de Lopez might expect of her,

Cañuela knew that he would certainly not imagine she would know "Lunfardo."

"So you live in Buenos Aires, *Sigñorita,*" Ramón de Lopez remarked.

Now he too was speaking Italian, but the pure and more cultured Italian of the aristocrats.

"Si, Sigñor."

Cañuela hoped that he would not ask her many questions. Anyway it would be incorrect at Carnival-time to try to discover the identity of one's partner.

The fun of the fiesta was to be anonymous! For a husband not to be aware of what his wife was wearing so that perhaps she would flirt with him unawares.

For an Argentine lady it was always a chance to capture a new suitor or to discover an unexpected admirer.

As if her thoughts somehow communicated themselves to Ramón de Lopez they danced in silence and Cañuela knew that because he partnered her so well, she was dancing in a manner that was almost faultless.

Ramón de Lopez did not lead her into the steps which her mother had said would shock the Dowagers, but as if he realised how proficient she was they executed more and more intricate and difficult figures.

'And yet,' Cañuela thought proudly, 'I have not made a mistake.'

Finally the dance came to an end and she felt Ramón de Lopez take her arm just below the elbow and lead her through the crowds into the garden.

Because she was bemused and at the same time excited by the dance she did not realise where he was taking her, until suddenly she found herself on one of the narrow, light-edged paths where they seemed to have left the crowds behind.

Instinctively Cañuela stopped and looked up at him.

"You dance very beautifully, *Sigñorita,*" he said in his deep voice.

"Grazie," she replied, her voice low, in fact hardly above a whisper.

He did not speak again and suddenly it seemed to Cañuela that his silence was full of meaning—a meaning she did not understand.

He was looking down at her and she felt that he was overpowering, overwhelming as he had been when he had come into her cabin and seemed too big for it.

"We must go . . . back," she said hesitatingly.

"If that is your wish," he replied.

He was still looking at her, seeking, she thought uncomfortably, to see behind her mask; to guess who she might be.

But he did not move and Cañuela felt as if her feet were rooted to the ground.

Then unexpectedly he reached out and took her hand in his.

"Thank you," he said very quietly and kissed it.

She felt the warm, hard pressure of his lips on her skin and was aware that a strange sensation like a streak of quicksilver ran through her body.

Then almost as if something beyond themselves commanded them they turned and walked back towards the crowd-filled garden.

As they reached the first group of people standing chatting with glasses of champagne in their hands, a figure dressed as La Dame aux Camélias detached herself with a little cry.

She ran to Ramón de Lopez and, putting out both her hands in their lace mittens, said in a low, intimate tone:

"I have been looking for you—waiting for you."

There was a note of passion in her voice that was unmistakable.

Without waiting to hear Ramón de Lopez's answer Cañuela moved swiftly away and without looking back walked through the crowds on the lawn towards the house.

She entered through one of the open doors and, finding the vestibule empty, slipped up the stairs without anyone seeing her.

She reached her own room, shut the door behind her, and pulled the sombrero from her head.

She felt as if her whole body was still throbbing with the music and the wonder of the dance.

They had tangoed together!

Whatever happened now, no-one could take that away from her.

She had danced as she had always wanted to dance and with a man whose steps matched hers and who moved with an expertise which she acknowledged was exceptional.

Slowly Cañuela took off Dolores's bright red skirt, black bodice, and embroidered blouse.

She put on her night-gown and loosened her hair so that it fell over her shoulders.

Far away in the distance she thought she could still hear the throb of the music.

She got into bed to lie in the dark, thinking over what had happened.

She had not realised how closely a man would hold a woman when they tangoed. There had been something secretly intimate about feeling her breast against his.

They had been close—so close that she had been half-afraid he would hear her heart beating.

Only now it seemed strange that they had said so little to each other.

Yet it would, Cañuela knew, have been difficult to talk when one was doing the difficult, complicated, and graceful steps of the tango.

But surely if she had been an ordinary partner of Ramón de Lopez she would have found a great deal to say to him.

She would have tried to entice him, as "La Dame aux Camélias" was undoubtedly doing at this moment.

She would have pouted her red lips as Señora Sánchez had done. She would have thrown back her head to reveal the long, rounded whiteness of her neck.

But Cañuela had done none of these things.

She had felt shy because, although Ramón de Lopez would have no idea who she might be, she was vividly conscious of him.

There was a strong, overpowering masculinity about him. It had disturbed her when they were working together and she had told herself it made her hate him.

But now she was not so sure.

She felt too that her hand was branded with his kiss.

"I was wrong to go to his Ball," Cañuela told herself. "He was a traitor to Papa and I hate him because of it."

But somehow in the darkness of her room she could only feel his lips on her hand.

Because her conscience was pricking her for the manner in which she had behaved the night before, Cañuela was down extra early the following morning.

Some letters and quite a number of cablegrams had arrived and lay on her desk.

She opened and deciphered them. She was wondering at what time Ramón de Lopez would send for her when Señor Náon came into the room.

"Buenos dias, Señorita," he said. "I hope you passed a restful night and were not kept awake by the music?"

"No, indeed, thank you, Señor. I slept well," Cañuela replied, regardless of the fact that it was not the truth.

"That is good," he said, "and now I see you are ready for work."

"I am indeed," Cañuela answered. "Is the Señor in his office?"

"No, he has gone riding this morning."

Señor Náon smiled and added:

"Usually when the Señor has had a late night he 'blows away the cob-webs,' as you say in your language, by riding hard. He says it is good for the liver!"

"That is what my father always used to say!" Cañuela exclaimed.

She realised as she spoke that she had given information about herself, which was something she had intended never to do.

"Your father was fond of horses?" Señor Náon enquired.

"Like most Englishmen," Cañuela said coldly. "I hope Señor Lopez will not be long. There are some cablegrams from England which require a reply."

Señor Náon smiled.

"The Señor is a law unto himself. Besides, he may find the ordinary routes out of the city are blocked this morning."

Cañuela looked surprised and Señor Náon went on:

"There was some rioting last night and the *Unión*

Civica Radical have put up barricades in some places whch have not yet been cleared away by the Police."

"There was trouble?" Cañuela asked.

"Little more than usual. I do not know whether you have heard about this new revolutionary element we have in Buenos Aires."

Cañuela had heard about them but she felt it wiser not to say so, and instead she said:

"You say there are revolutionaries? That sounds frightening!"

"It all began four years ago, in 1889," Señor Náon said, obviously pleased to be able to explain to Cañuela something about which he thought she knew nothing. "And started with the denunciations of the scandals of the *nouveaux riches* by members of the old entrenched aristocracy."

"I thought you said they were revolutionaries?"

"They were a few disgruntled and disillusioned members of Society who found something in common with the discontent and bitterness of the wage-workers," Señor Náon explained.

"So they formed an organisation?" Cañuela suggested.

She was aware that she must ask questions.

"It is a political organisation," Señor Náon replied, "called the *Unión Civica Radical*, and they rallied the people in protestations and outbreaks of violence."

"Did they succeed?" Cañuela enquired.

"They caused everyone a lot of trouble," the Señor replied. "There were big, popular demonstrations in the streets and they initiated a movement in opposition to the Government, which had the support of the Navy."

"The Navy defected?" Cañuela enquired with surprise.

"It was its capacity to shell Government troops, which caused the President to reconsider his position. He tried to cling to office, but it was hopeless and he resigned."

Cañuela was genuinely surprised.

She had heard of the *Unión Civica* before she had left Buenos Aires, but she had not realised how strong it had grown or that it was in fact a large enough party to be considered seriously.

Señor Náon sighed.

"Of course, as always happens with these things," he said, "there is a rowdy element which gets out of hand, and that is what happened last night."

"What did they do?" Cañuela asked.

"Smashed the windows of Government buildings, caused a lot of trouble for the Police, and were responsible, needless to say, for several deaths."

Cañuela knew that this was nothing new for Independence Day.

At the same time she could not help remembering how dangerous revolutionaries could be when they fought fanatically against law and order.

"Let us hope that Señor Lopez does not encounter any opposition on his ride."

"That I feel is very unlikely," Señor Náon replied, "but I should not be too impatient for his return, Señorita. He might, if he feels like it, go as far as the *Estancia*."

"Surely that is two hours' ride from here?" Cañuela cried almost in dismay.

"I doubt if the Señor will take so long," Señor Naon said with a smile. "On the other hand he might return at any moment."

It was the typical Argentine attitude, Cañuela thought.

After a little while she gave up watching the door impatiently for Ramón de Lopez's return, and, having left word as to where she could be found, went into the garden.

A large number of servants were clearing up the débris from the night before.

Flowers were being taken away from the Ball-Room, dirty glasses and plates were being collected.

A number of gardeners were taking down the lanterns from the trees and removing the fairy-lights from the paths.

Unconscious of where her feet were carrying her, Cañuela found herself walking along the narrow path she had walked with Ramón de Lopez.

Why when the dance was over had they said so little to each other?

Could it be that he was feeling the same magic that she had while their steps moved in unison?

She recognised now that it had been an unexpected enchantment that she could dance the tango with him so well that she had not for a moment hesitated or stumbled, or even had to worry as to what her next step would be.

"We were perfectly matched!" she told herself.

Then hastily, because she did not wish to think of him anymore, she went back into the house.

She tidied the office, which she had already tidied before, and finally taking up a book on economics she tried to read.

But she was conscious all the time that she was listening for her employer's return, anxious, she told herself, to know what reply he wished to give to the cablegrams which had come from England.

Her luncheon was served in the same small room overlooking the court-yard where she had dined on her first night.

Through the open windows she could see the beautiful marble carving on the fountain and hear the soft sound of its water rising towards the sky and falling again into the marble basin.

She found herself watching it, and yet she still had the feeling that she was waiting and listening.

Impatient with herself, Cañuela sat down and wrote a long letter to her mother.

She tried to remember every little detail that she thought would be of interest to her—what Buenos Aires looked like, a description of Ramón de Lopez's house, the gaiety of the Ball last night.

"I danced with Señor Lopez . . ." she began, then crossed out the words.

She could not say why, but she did not want her mother to know that they had danced together.

She finished the letter, addressed it, stamped it, and left it with the post to be collected.

It was four o'clock when Señor Náon entered the office.

He would have had a *siesta,* Cañuela knew, after luncheon, which would fill up at least two hours of his day.

"There is no sign of Señor de Lopez as yet," he said. "He must, as I anticipated, have gone to the *Estancia.* I am surprised, because I had expected him to go there tomorrow."

"Perhaps he was anxious to see that everyone was back at work," Cañuela said with a smile. "I imagine they too like everybody else celebrated Independence Day."

"The little village will have been decorated," Señor Náon replied, "and there will have been fire-works provided by Señor Lopez. Everybody there is of course employed by him."

"Are there many of them?" Cañuela asked.

"Over two hundred," the Señor replied. "The village is a model of its kind, built round an old Church."

"I hope I shall be able to see it one day," Cañuela said.

"I am sure that the Señor will wish you to accompany him to the *Estancia,*" Señor Náon said, but his voice lacked conviction.

As she was about to reply the door was flung open and one of the house-servants entered.

There was a strange expression on his face as he ejaculated:

"Señor Náon, it is Alberto. He has returned!"

"Alberto?" Señor Náon exclaimed.

Into the office came a man dressed in the smart outfit of the *gaucho* who is in private service.

"Señor Náon!" he exclaimed, "you will not believe—you cannot imagine what has happened, but I was told to come back and bring you this note. And you must act—you must act at once!"

"What is all this about?" Señor Náon asked in alarm.

"The Señor—they have taken him. There were at least fifteen of them. There was nothing we could do—nothing!"

Cañuela rose to her feet.

She saw Alberto hand Señor Náon a piece of paper which he took and read slowly.

Cañuela could not restrain herself.

"What has happened? What is it?"

"It is the guerrillas, Señorita," Alberto replied. "The guerrillas of the *Unión Civica*. They have taken the Señor prisoner."

"I cannot believe it!" Cañuela cried incredulously.

As she spoke Señor Náon handed her the piece of paper Alberto had given him.

She saw at once that it was in Señor Lopez's handwriting and for a moment the words danced in front of her eyes before she read:

> *I have been taken prisoner by members of the* Unión Civica. *They demand a ransom of one million pesos, half of which must be in gold. They inform me that if the money is not handed over by twelve noon tomorrow, I shall be shot. Alberto has instructions as to where to contact them.*
>
> *Ramón de Lopez.*

Cañuela read the note slowly and felt as though the words would not percolate her mind.

"It cannot be true! This is impossible!" Señor Náon exclaimed.

"It is true, Señor," Alberto assured him miserably. "They came upon us unexpectedly. We were riding home from the *Estancia*. We had been galloping hard, for the Señor had a new horse."

He made an expressive gesture with his hands.

"Even if the horses had been fresh, we could not have got away. They came towards us and at first we did not realise who they might be."

"You say there were fifteen of them?" Señor Náon asked.

"About fifteen, Señor, perhaps more. I did not count. I was so agitated, so frightened! They encircled us."

"What did the Señor do?"

"He asked them what they wanted," Alberto answered. "They talked with him for a long time. I did not think it was anything serious. I thought they were asking the Señor's help."

"I can understand that," Señor Náon interposed. "How could you suppose that the Señor, of all people, should be in danger?"

"They said their quarrel was not with him personally," Alberto explained, "but that they must have money. They had therefore decided to kidnap the first rich man they saw riding unprotected outside the city."

"You had pistols with you?" Cañuela asked.

"There were two of us, Señorita," Alberto answered, "only two! Besides, when they were all round us there would have been no point in dying."

He paused to say dramatically:

"We would have killed perhaps two of them, and they would have killed us!"

It was an unanswerable argument and Cañuela said:

"What happened when the Señor understood what they wanted?"

"He was very quiet and calm, Señorita. He told them it would do no good, but they would not listen."

"What happened then?" Señor Náon enquired.

"They said they must have a million pesos, and it was the Señor who suggested that I should bring back the note."

"He was saving you from being taken prisoner," Cañuela said.

"I realise that, Señorita, but I would much rather have gone with him," Alberto replied. "But he said no, I was to come back, give the note to Señor Náon, and he would know what to do."

"I should know what to do?" Señor Náon shouted. "But what shall I do? How can I give them a million pesos? That rabble—that scum! They will use it to buy up more arms to kill more people!"

"Could not the Military do something?" Cañuela asked.

Señor Náon shook his head.

"They would attack the guerrillas if they knew where to find them," he answered, "but the Pampas stretches far and wide and a rabble like this can hide anywhere."

"Have the guerrillas done this before?" Cañuela asked.

"Last year they kidnapped a politician," Señor Náon replied. "He was a poor man and the Party did not consider him of much consequence. When the money did not arrive, day by day they sent one of his fingers back to the city."

"Oh no!" Cañuela cried.

"Finally the money was collected," Señor Náon continued, "but the unfortunate victim will always be five fingers short!"

"It is horrible . . . terrible! . . . terrible!" Cañuela murmured.

She thought of how Ramón de Lopez's fingers had touched hers last night and the strange feeling she had felt when they danced together.

It was unbearable to think of his being mutilated. She drew a deep breath.

"You must find the money immediately, Señor Náon!" she insisted. "It is really not such an astronomical sum where the Señor is concerned."

"I suppose not," Señor Náon answered. "I will go to the Bank and explain what has happened."

"There is one more thing that the men said to me as I was leaving," Alberto said.

"What was that?" Cañuela asked.

"They said: 'Come alone with the money. If you bring soldiers or the Police with you, we will kill the Señor.' "

"That is what we might have expected," Cañuela said in a low voice.

"It is disgraceful!" Señor Náon exclaimed, "disgraceful that in this day and age a civilised country should experience such outrages!"

His voice rang out as he continued:

"They are a disgrace to themselves—a disgrace to their own Party! To give them money will only make it easier for them to commit more crimes—more and more until none of us are safe!"

"In the meantime we must save the Señor!" Cañuela said quietly.

"I will go to the Bank."

Señor Náon turned towards the door but Cañuela stopped him.

"I should not say too much about what has happened," she suggested, "except perhaps to the Bank manager himself."

Señor Náon waited and she went on:

"There is always the chance that members of the Government might think like you, that to give in to the guerrillas is to encourage them. They might insist on sending the Military to try and save the Señor—in which case he would die!"

"I see your point," Señor Náon said. "I will swear the Bank manager to secrecy. On his return perhaps Señor de Lopez will have ideas about how these men can be brought to heel."

He paused and then he said:

"I hope that after they receive the money they will in fact release him."

Cañuela drew in her breath.

She had not thought of that.

She had known only that nothing mattered except that Ramón de Lopez should be free.

Señor Náon left the room and Alberto stood for a moment looking at Cañuela.

She had the feeling that he was trying to find words in which to explain to her that he had not been a coward—he had not drawn his pistol simply because it had been hopeless.

She knew only too well that it was the pride of the *gauchos* that they never accepted defeat. They would be killed rather than surrender!

Before he could speak she said quietly:

"I know there was nothing you could do, Alberto."

"I would die for the Señor—do you hear me, Señorita? I would die for him! But when I would have drawn my pistol he said: 'No, Alberto,' and I knew that he meant it."

"I am sure he did," Cañuela said. "It would have been senseless to throw away your life."

"Thank you, Señorita, for understanding," Alberto said.

He would have left the room but Cañuela stopped him by saying:

"Where do you think they will take him, Alberto? Where will they hide him?"

Alberto shrugged his shoulders.

"There are many places, Señorita, by the marshes, near the River or the sea."

"If there were fifteen of them," Cañuela said, "and the Señor makes sixteen, that is quite a crowd. Even the high grass of the Pampas would not conceal them completely."

"That is true, Señorita," Alberto said. "But I do not think they would go to the Pampas. That scum would want to cook a meal. They would want to rest their horses. They will have a hide-out somewhere."

"Yes . . . but where?" Cañuela asked.

Again Alberto made a gesture with his hands and would have turned again towards the door.

"When you left the Señor," Cañuela said, "you rode away from him towards the city. Did you look back?"

"*Si*, Señorita, I looked back and I saw them riding away with the Señor in the centre of them. I expect they were afraid he would try to escape."

"I am sure they were," Cañuela agreed. "In which direction were they going? East or West?"

"When I looked back the first time they were going South, Señorita, and then when I looked a second time they were far, far away in the distance, but they had turned East."

Cañuela drew in her breath.

She knew as Alberto spoke almost as if someone told her so where the guerrillas were taking Ramón de Lopez. She knew with a conviction which had something almost clairvoyant about it.

"Listen, Alberto," she said in a low voice, "are you prepared to come with me tonight to try to rescue the Señor?"

He looked at her, his dark eyes wide with astonishment.

"Rescue him, Señorita? But we do not know where they have taken him."

"I think I know . . . I am sure I know," Cañuela

said, "but it would be a mistake to tell anyone else in the household what we are going to do. They might try to stop us."

"You mean that you and I, Señorita, can rescue him?" Alberto asked incredulously.

"You and I alone, Alberto," Cañuela replied. "Because it would be dangerous for more than two of us to approach the guerrillas' hiding-place, we must go alone."

"Do you not think, Señorita, that you should inform Señor Náon?"

"We will tell no-one!" Cañuela said firmly. "And you must give me your word of honour, Alberto, that you will keep silent. I promise you that it is the only way we can save the Señor."

"If it is to save the Señor I will do anything!" Alberto said. "Anything!"

He paused, then added dejectedly:

"I know what the others will say to me when they hear. They will say I was a coward to have left him. That I should have killed those who took him prisoner."

"You did what was right and what the Señor wanted you to do, and now I want your help. I know I can trust you."

"I will do what you say, Señorita."

"Then go and rest," Cañuela said. "When it is dark I will meet you at the stables. Do not tell anyone what we are about to do. We shall need three horses."

"Three, Señorita?"

"One for you, one for me, and one for the Señor on which he can ride home."

Alberto groaned.

"I hope you are right, Señorita. To bring him home without having to pay the ransom money would be a great triumph!"

"It is not a question of money," Cañuela said, "but of letting the guerrillas succeed in their wicked scheme—or of defeating them!"

"You think we can defeat them, Señorita?"

"If it is humanly possible," Cañuela replied, "you and I will bring the Señor home with us tonight."

She saw Alberto's eyes light up and then she added:

"Not one word, Alberto, to anyone. You understand? Everything will depend upon your keeping silent."

"On the sacred heart of Jesus, not one word will cross my lips!"

"Then I will come to the stables as soon as it is dark."

Alberto saluted her and went from the room.

Only when he had gone did Cañuela realise that she was trembling.

Somehow it did not seem believable that Ramón de Lopez could have been taken prisoner by revolutionaries; that he should be humiliated into giving in to their demands.

And that even when the money was paid, there was no guarantee that they would not kill him.

He had seen the men and would know who they were.

Would they under the circumstances be willing to let him go, knowing that if they were captured their freedom, if not their lives, would be forfeit?

'I must find him! I must save him!' Cañuela thought to herself.

She went up to her bed-room.

Dolores had unpacked all her trunks, and opening her wardrobe she found two riding-habits.

One had belonged to her mother and was a very elegant outfit cut by a London tailor, in which Mrs. Arlington had evoked admiration every time she appeared on horse-back.

The other was one Cañuela had worn as a girl.

It was fashioned Mexican-style in dark green suede, and the fringed suede skirt was divided so that she could ride astride.

It would have been most impracticable on her long expeditions with her father to ride side-saddle or to be encumbered with a full skirt, which was far more suitable for a lady trotting in the Park.

With the divided skirt there was a silk shirt and a sleeveless waist-coat also of fringed suede.

Cañuela knew that she was really too old now to wear such an outfit.

At the same time it was important that she should

travel swiftly and not be encumbered by a fashionable riding-habit.

Because she knew how urgent and exhausting the next few hours would prove, she forced herself to lie down on her bed.

She would want all her strength for what lay ahead.

She found herself praying that she would be able to rescue Ramón de Lopez.

It was hard to think of him as a prisoner; even more terrifying to think of him being mutilated; his fingers cut off by rough, brutal men who perhaps would enjoy watching him suffer.

'It must not happen to him . . . it must not!' Cañuela prayed.

He was so proud, so autocratic—even to imagine him at the mercy of the guerrillas was unthinkable.

Once again Cañuela wondered if they would let him go.

Last night he had seemed overwhelming . . . overpowering . . . as they had walked together along the light-edged path.

Her heart had been beating quickly, just as it had done when they had danced together, and she had been aware of how close they were.

She had been acutely conscious then of his closeness, and yet in the garden, when he was no longer touching her, he had seemed just as close.

Tomorrow he might be dead!

It was not conceivable—and yet it could happen!

"I must save him . . . I must!" Cañuela told herself. "Oh, God, help me! Help me!"

Her fingers tightened together with the intensity of her prayer and then as she saw that they were white from the pressure she knew why she felt so desperate! Why the thought of Ramón de Lopez a prisoner was like a dagger in her heart.

She loved him!

She loved him, but love had crept secretly upon her and she had not been aware of it.

For a moment she could hardly believe that it was true; that she was not just dramatising the situation and imagining her own emotions.

Then she knew that she had loved him for a long time.

She had loved him when they sat fencing with each other over the table in the Dining-Saloon or discussing the papers strewn about in the cabin.

She had loved him when, holding the sleeping baby in her arms, she had looked up and seen an expression in his eyes which had made her feel as if her breath was caught in her throat.

She had loved him last night when they had danced together, and the feeling when his hand had touched hers had not been fear but . . . love!

"How stupid of me not to know it!" Cañuela said to herself.

Then with an agony that was like a bullet searing its way through her body she knew that her love was a thing of shame.

How could she possibly love a man who had betrayed her father? Who had failed him, who had turned Judas on his friend!

Ramón de Lopez was a traitor! The man she had hated! The man she had longed to see humbled and humiliated.

But now she loved him!

And she knew almost despairingly that she must save him, even if she herself died in the attempt.

SEVEN

After the bright lights of the city the open country seemed dark until gradually Cañuela found her eyes getting used to it.

The stars were coming out and over the vast, flat land the expanse of the Heavens seemed immense as it stretched towards a limitless horizon.

The going was good, and yet they could not ride fast as Alberto had not only to control his own horse but the spare mount he had brought for Ramón de Lopez.

Cañuela was well aware that Alberto thought her optimistic in saying that the Señor would be returning with them.

At the same time he was desperately anxious not only for his master's safety, but to save his own face from the innuendo that he had played the coward.

She was however not prepared to concern herself with Alberto's feelings but to wonder agonisingly if she was right in her guess as to where Ramón de Lopez might be.

Her father had been intensely interested in the ruins of the Jesuit Missions which had been established in the territory towards the middle of the seventeenth century.

They had visited many of these ancient ruins when travelling about Argentina.

The most important were to be found in Misiones, but there were a number of others and one in particular near the city of Buenos Aires.

Lionel Arlington had explained that in Argentina the Spaniards had found conquest and colonisation difficult because the Indians were hunters—not husbandmen and craftsmen.

They were also fleet of foot, and the open Pampas, where they could run as fast as ostriches, made it easy for them to escape from their masters.

It was therefore essential for the Spaniards to build themselves places where the Indians could be kept more or less as slaves and forced to work under sharp-eyed overseers.

The Jesuit Missions were therefore small towns in themselves, surrounded by walls which could be guarded.

They contained besides Monasteries or Convents with their long galleries, quarters where the Indian labourers were imprisoned.

Cañuela had been entranced by the beauty of the ruins which still remained.

The elegance of the columns and the complicated filigree stone engravings all were achievements of marvellous Indian craftsmanship.

The ruins to which she was going now and in which she was certain the guerrillas would have made their headquarters was in an isolated place far away from any main road.

She and her father had discovered it quite by chance on one of their rides.

It lay on the centre of thick thorn hedges through which it was impossible for a man or horse to pass.

But they had discovered a way through it and Cañuela realised now how easy it would be for one or two men to guard the entrance and know ostensibly there was no other way to approach the ruins.

Years of research had taught Lionel Arlington that the Indian slaves had their own method of escaping from their conquerors.

The lure of the Pampas was stronger than their fear of being killed or tortured, and in some places the Spaniards conceded defeat, finding that they could not carry on with an ever-disappearing labour-force.

"How did they get away, Papa?" Cañuela had asked.

"When they were carving the pilasters, bases, and pedestals which make the Jesuit buildings so outstanding, they also tunnelled themselves a way of escape, and they needed it!"

"It must have been dangerous for them," Cañuela said.

"Discovery would have meant instant death and that must have happened in innumerable cases," Lionel Arlington replied. "But we can still find in some of the ruins the passages through which the Indians could reach their beloved Pampas."

"Please show me one, Papa!" Cañuela had begged.

"We have to find it first," Lionel Arlington answered good-humouredly.

It had taken no less than eight visits to the ruins outside Buenos Aires before Lionel Arlington had discovered what he sought.

They had gone back in triumph to tell Mrs. Arlington of their success, and she had promised that one day she would accompany them to see the secret tunnel of which they were so proud.

But before she could do so the scandal of her husband's supposed treachery had broken and they had left for England.

Remembering the plan of the ruins, Cañuela was certain that Ramón de Lopez would be placed in what had originally been the Indian quarters.

The walls there were thicker or perhaps they were stronger because they were not decorated, and had withstood the onslaught of time.

It was a large room almost the shape of an oblong box, roofless but with an opening onto what had been a main court-yard of the Mission.

It would have been easy to guard and impossible for a man imprisoned there to escape unless he was equipped to climb up a twenty-foot wall, which even when he scaled it would bring him only to the thorn hedge outside.

"That is where the Señor will be!" Cañuela told herself and then felt a throb of fear in case they had already hurt or tortured him.

She was afraid for him with a pain that was a physical agony in her breast.

Even while she told herself that such feelings were wrong and a betrayal of her love for her father, she knew that nothing could prevent her from feeling them.

"How could I have been so foolish," she asked herself, "as not to realise that to be alone, as I have been, with the most attractive man in Argentina made it inevitable that I should fall in love with him?"

Could anything be more hopeless than to love a man who had every woman in the country ready to fall into his arms even before he asked it of them?

To him she was nothing but a superior servant.

As she had told him, she was well aware of her position in his hierarchy.

In many ways the Argentines had carried on the rigid, formal protocol of their Spanish ancestors.

A Spaniard would never lower his pride by marrying a social inferior, and the great Argentine families married amongst themselves and were far more proud of their ancestral tree than any English aristocrat.

Riding into the night, Cañuela asked herself savagely:

"Why should I think of marriage?"

She was well aware that marriage as far as she was concerned was impossible.

She had faced the fact before and even to think of marriage in connection with Ramón de Lopez was laughable.

She was an outcast—a pariah—the daughter of a Diplomat who had been accused of treachery to his own country, and because of that she could never be the wife of any decent man.

"But I love him! I love him!" her heart told her despairingly.

Because of the pain of it she spurred her horse on faster until she realised that Alberto was getting left behind.

They had ridden for nearly an hour when Cañuela drew in her reins, and as Alberto did likewise she had a moment of panic.

Supposing she had forgotten the way?

Supposing alone she could not find what she was seeking?

Then a little ahead she saw, as she had expected, the dark shadow of some bushes by a boulder which looked as if it had been thrown there by a giant hand.

This was where she planned to leave the horses.

She rode up to the bushes and gave the reins of her horse to Alberto, who had already dismounted.

"Stay here!" she said in a whisper, "and keep very quiet. Sounds travel."

She knew that he would be aware of this and he did not answer her but made a movement of his head to show that he understood.

She walked away over the rough scrub-land where the high grasses would not grow, but where she knew in the day-time she would see the flowers of penny-royal, wild thyme, and flowering bean.

She moved on to where the ground grew rougher and there was a slight incline.

The Mission had been built on a hill, not a very high one in this part of the country, but nevertheless it rose above the surrounding land.

At the foot of the natural rise Cañuela searched for what she and her father had found three years ago.

The opening was obscured by clumps of grass and the coarse vegetation which was profuse at this time of the year.

But the stones with which she and her father had blocked and concealed the exit they had discovered were still there.

She pulled them away one by one, careful not to make a noise, until in front of her was a dark opening, just large enough for a man to crawl through.

Cañuela had attached a lantern to her saddle.

It had been difficult to procure and finally she had had to ask Dolores to find her one.

It was the type of small lantern that shepherds or farmers carried at night, containing only the stump of a thick candle which was protected when lit by strong glass.

She crawled through the small opening, protecting the lantern with her body, and after she had proceeded two or three yards she was able to sit on the ground and light it.

As she remembered, the roof of the passage here was higher and enabled a man to walk along it if he kept his back bent.

Roughly hewn from the rocks, it must have been a tremendous achievement to burrow so far beneath the earth with the inadequate tools which were all the craftsman had at the time.

Because of their skill, the passage had withstood the passing of three centuries, and carrying her lantern in her hand Cañuela moved slowly along it.

Her back was beginning to ache as she climbed upwards all the way until finally in front of her she saw the passage narrow down again to a small opening similar to the one by which she had entered.

She inspected it very carefully, and found the lever which her father had shown her would move a large stone at the base of a wall inside the room in the Mission where the slaves were kept.

It has been so skillfully contrived that from the inside it was impossible to discern.

The large stone which opened on the tunnel was identical to the other large stones at the base of the wall.

But this one was on a pivot.

Only Lionel Arlington's persistence and the fact that his previous discoveries had shown him where to look had resulted in their finding the escape route of the Indians.

The lever had rusted with the years, but they had cleaned and oiled it until it moved quite freely.

Now Cañuela could only pray that since she and her father had been here it had not once again become stiff.

If it had, she doubted if she would be able to move it single-handed.

She set down the lantern and pushing the lever with both hands she felt it give a little.

She was tense as she did so, in case after all she had planned she would be defeated at the very last moment.

But now she was certain that she could move the stone, and the only thing that remained was to find if she had been correct in her guess as to where Ramón de Lopez was hidden.

She blew out the lantern and, pushing the lever, as

her father had shown her how to do, she felt the great stone move forward.

Then she heard voices.

There were men talking, there was coarse laughter, and it was followed unexpectedly by the sound of a guitar.

Cañuela drew in her breath.

Nothing could be better!

If there were any sound from the stone the music would drown it.

It was heavy and very thick but by using all her strength she managed to push it open a little further.

Now it was possible to see lights and smell the smoke from a fire and the tang of raw tobacco.

She looked through the aperture which she had made, which was hardly more than an inch wide.

To the right she could first see the guerrillas seated round an open fire they had kindled in the courtyard.

The flames revealed their faces, coarse, rough, and unshaven. Some of the men were lifting bottles to their mouths or eating food that had been cooked over the fire.

Very slowly Cañuela opened the stone a little further.

Now she looked frontwards and felt herself start as she saw Ramón de Lopez.

He was sitting in the dark against the wall almost opposite her.

Even on the floor with his legs stretched out in their high boots he looked elegant and unbelievably at his ease.

She wondered what he was thinking about, for it seemed to her that he was completely unconscious of the men laughing and joking round the fire.

She pushed the stone a little further and as she did so realised that a guard with a gun across his knees was seated against an outside wall looking towards the fire.

He had his back to her just the other side of the opening into the room.

It would have been impossible for anyone to pass

from what made a natural prison without his being aware of it.

Cañuela opened the stone still further.

Now she could put her head and shoulders through it.

She was looking straight at Ramón de Lopez and she was aware that he, deep in his thoughts, did not see her or in fact show any interest in what was happening round him.

She wondered how to attract his attention. Then she felt that her thoughts must communicate themselves to him.

If she willed him to think of her, surely the mere fact that she was there must in some way impress itself on his consciousness.

She looked at him and because she could not help herself she found herself saying beneath her breath:

"I love you! I love you!"

It was almost as if she spoke the words aloud, for instantly she attracted his attention.

She saw him stiffen, his head rise, but he was wise enough not to move sharply or do anything for the moment but stare in her direction.

She held out her hand and beckoned. Then she moved backwards so that the aperture was there, dark and empty, and he would understand.

This was the dangerous moment and she held her breath.

Ramón de Lopez rose slowly to his feet.

He yawned and stretched.

At his first movement the guard turned his head.

"The ground in this place is damned hard!" Ramón de Lopez remarked in a grumbling tone.

"What do you expect, Señor," the guard replied, "a feather bed?"

He laughed scornfully.

"I would certainly prefer it," Ramón de Lopez answered.

"Perhaps I'll buy you one with the million pesos when they arrive tomorrow," the guard said sarcastically.

"Maybe I will keep you to that promise," Ramón de Lopez replied.

He walked casually across to lean against the wall nearest the opening, then slowly he lowered himself onto the floor, making quite a noise with his boots.

The music from the guitar grew louder and the man playing it began to sing a bawdy song.

The others joined in.

The guard picked up a bottle which lay beside him and lifted it to his lips.

As he did so Ramón de Lopez with incredible swiftness turned from where he was sitting and with the litheness of a snake slipped through the hole left by the open stone.

There was just room enough for him to ease his broad shoulders through it, and even as he crawled forward into the darkness Cañuela put out her hand, found his, and drew him further into the tunnel.

She slipped past him and, finding the lever, pulled the stone back into place.

It was difficult to close completely and she thought that she would have to ask his help.

But suddenly it slipped into position, just as it had done after her father had oiled it.

Now there was only darkness, but she could hear him breathing.

She crawled past him again and found the lantern.

She lit it and holding it up saw that he was sitting on the ground looking at her.

He looked very strong and handsome in the flickering light and there was an expression in his eyes which made her feel shy.

Without speaking, holding the lantern so that it was easy to see the way, she started back down the low passage.

She went slowly, well aware that for Ramón de Lopez it would be exceedingly uncomfortable.

The passage had been made for Indians who were very much smaller than he was and she knew that to follow her he must be almost doubled up.

But it was important that they should get away quickly.

When the guerrillas found that he had gone they would undoubtedly start to search the immediate neighbourhood.

They would suppose, although it would seem impossible, that he must somehow have climbed the wall, found his way through the thorn hedge, and reached the open country.

To be recaptured would be disastrous, Cañuela was only too well aware of that, and so she knew that they must waste no time.

Fortunately it was easier going back down the passage than it had been going up.

Yet it seemed to Cañuela to take a long time, although really it was only a few minutes, before they reached the narrow opening by which she had entered.

Through it was blowing a fresh, clean wind, and Cañuela put out the candle and closed the little door of the lantern.

When she had done so she would have gone first through the opening, but to her surprise she felt Ramón de Lopez's hands on her shoulders.

He set her to one side and went ahead of her.

She realised that he had done this so that, if there was any danger waiting for them, he would be the first to encounter it.

Following him, she could see him silhouetted against the stars.

She crawled after him into the opening and found his hand waiting to take hers.

He pulled her to her feet. Then as she stood up he put his arms round her and his mouth was on hers.

She had been so intent on taking him to safety that his action took her completely by surprise.

For a moment she was still from sheer astonishment, before she became aware of the warm insistence of his lips.

Instinctively her hands went up as if to struggle against him.

Then she felt something so strange, so wonderful, shoot through her that it was an ecstasy beyond words.

She could not explain. It was like no feeling she had ever known before.

It was a wonder and a rapture, something so incredibly marvellous that she felt as if her whole being flared into life.

He held her closer and still closer until she melted into him and he was part of the night and the stars, and they were one person.

Then, when the earth was no longer solid beneath her feet, the world had vanished and she could think of nothing but him, he released her.

Taking her hand, he drew her quickly towards the boulder where the horses were hidden.

He must have known that that was where they would be, Canuela thought afterwards, because he did not ask her where to go and she was incapable of speech.

She had not known that a kiss could be so unbelievably, miraculously wonderful!

She felt as if she throbbed and glowed with a mystical radiance because his mouth had possessed her.

Still hand in hand, they reached the boulder and behind it they found Alberto waiting with the three horses.

"Señor!" Alberto exclaimed in an incredulous whisper.

"Shush!" Ramón de Lopez admonished.

He picked Cañuela up in his arms and lifted her into the saddle.

He mounted his horse and in the space of a few seconds they were all three galloping away with a swiftness which told Cañuela all too clearly that they knew they were still in danger.

It was fortunate that Ramón de Lopez's horses were of the finest blood-stock, while she felt certain that those used by the guerrillas, unless they had stolen them, were of very inferior breed.

At the same time she knew that he feared, as she did, that at any moment they might hear bullets whistling after them and the guerrillas would come galloping from the ruins.

They had ridden well over a mile before Ramón de Lopez turned his head and Cañuela did likewise.

It was difficult to see in the starlit darkness whether anyone was following them.

It was easy to be deceived by shadows; by the movement of the wind in the grasses.

Without speaking they turned their faces once again and set off at a speed which precluded all possible conversation even had they wished to make it.

Cañuela felt that she had never been so glad to see anything as she was to see the lights of Buenos Aires.

They meant security, safety, and that Ramón de Lopez was no longer in danger!

Even now she could hardly bear to think that he might have been killed or mutilated by the men she had seen sitting round the fire.

And she would never be sure if, even when the money had been turned over to them, Ramón de Lopez would have escaped with his life.

There was no honour amongst those sort of thieves and Cañuela was certain that they would not have run the risk of being hunted with a price on their heads, and with their faces known to the man they had captured.

At last they were riding through the cobbled streets of the city.

There were few people about at this time of the night and it was not long before they reached the Plaza St. Martin.

Ramón de Lopez dismounted at the front door of his house.

As he did so the door was flung open, a golden light came streaming forth, and Señor Náon surrounded by most of the members of the household staff came crowding out onto the steps.

They must have discovered, Cañuela thought, that she had gone, and the fact that Alberto had taken three horses would have suggested their intentions.

There was no time for conjecture, for a great cry of welcome went up when the servants saw their master.

Ramón de Lopez was smiling in response as he lifted Cañuela down from the saddle and they walked together up the steps and into the big, cool Hall.

As usual when Argentines were excited, there was a tremendous noise.

Everyone was asking questions; everyone talking at once.

There was no formality and convention was forgotten. For the moment Ramón de Lopez was not their employer but a man like themselves who had been miraculously restored to them from danger.

"How did it happen, Señor? How did you manage it?" Señor Náon was asking over and over again. "I had the money ready for tomorrow! I cannot believe that you are here! That you have escaped."

"It was all due to Miss Gray," Ramón de Lopez replied.

As he spoke he realised that Cañuela had slipped away.

She hurried up the staircase and along the balcony to her room.

She did not wish to give any explanations; she did not want to tell Ramón de Lopez how she knew of the secret tunnel from the ruins.

She had thought all the way back to Buenos Aires how hard it would be to explain to him how she knew that the passage existed.

What could she say? What possible story could she concoct? And whatever she said, unless it was the truth, would he believe her?

She reached her own room and shut the door as if she was shutting out danger, but this time it was not for Ramón de Lopez but for herself.

She looked down at her riding-habit and realised that it was covered with dust from crawling through the opening to the passage.

Her hair was untidy and blown by the wind but as she looked in the mirror she realised that her eyes were very bright and her lips were red, soft, and tender.

"It is because he kissed me," she told herself.

At his kiss love had seemed to burst like a flame inside her.

She had not known that it was possible to have such feelings; to be carried away until she had forgotten everything except that his mouth was on hers.

She knew then that she must go away.

She could not stay in his house, wanting, as she had

never wanted anything in her whole life, for him to kiss her again.

She could not stay and see him turn from her in horror and perhaps disgust when he learnt that she was Lionel Arlington's daughter.

"I must go quickly," Cañuela told herself frantically.

Her trunks were kept in a wardrobe-room which opened off her bed-room.

It was where Dolores had unpacked them and they were stacked neatly against the wall, a cotton cover draped over them.

Cañuela locked the door of her bed-room and, taking off her dusty riding-habit, began to pack.

She had only just begun when there was a knock at the door.

She stiffened and then asked apprehensively:

"Who is it?"

"It is Dolores, Señorita. I have brought you some food and the Señor thought you would like something to drink."

"I am too tired, Dolores," Cañuela answered. "I am almost asleep."

"Then I will tell the Señor you do not wish to be disturbed."

"Say I am in bed."

"I will tell him, Señorita."

Cañuela heard Dolores's steps going away along the balcony and went on with her packing.

It was about three o'clock in the morning.

Cañuela planned to rest for an hour or so and then go to the Quay.

She knew that ships often left the harbour on the morning tide, sailing at about seven o'clock. She thought that if she arrived at the port before six she would easily be able to obtain a berth.

It was fortunate that she had her return-ticket, and the money her mother had insisted on her bringing with her was still intact.

Cañuela lay down on her bed.

She had thought that she might sleep but she was too agitated.

At the same time something within her rebelled at

the thought of going away; of leaving Ramón de Lopez.

'I want to stay . . . I want to stay . . .' her heart throbbed over and over again.

But her brain told her that her only course was to leave, and leave at once.

It was unlikely that Ramón de Lopez would learn of her departure until he came down to breakfast, by which time she would be well on her way.

And yet because she was afraid that she might be discovered and prevented from leaving, Cañuela was dressed and ready soon after five o'clock.

Already the golden rays of the sun were streaming through the bed-room window; she knew that there would be some movement in the streets by now.

She rang the bell. It was nearly ten minutes before Dolores, looking astonished and still sleepy, answered it.

"You rang, Señorita?"

"I have to return to England immediately, Dolores," Cañuela said. "My mother is ill and needs me."

"I am sorry to hear that, Señorita, but what will the Señor say?"

"He will understand," Cañuela replied, "but you must help me, Dolores, I do not want to make a fuss. I just want one of the men-servants to carry my trunks downstairs and put them in a carriage."

"I will order one from the stables, Señorita."

"No . . . no. A hackney carriage will do," Cañuela said. "The fewer people are disturbed by my departure the better!"

Dolores looked at her in surprise but she did not question her further.

Instead she fetched two men who carried the trunks downstairs, and more quickly than Cañuela had dared to hope a hackney carriage was found, her luggage was piled onto it, and she set off for the Quay.

"The Señor is not to be told until he comes down to breakfast," Cañuela said firmly. "It might distress him that he could not say good-bye to me, and I have no wish to make any farewells."

"I can understand that, Señorita, if you are worried about your mother," Dolores said.

"Then please do as I ask," Cañuela insisted.

She gave Dolores one of her precious sovereigns and waved as she drove off in the carriage to the pretty Argentine girl who was standing on the steps beside the two men-servants.

"This is my good-bye," Cañuela told herself, "good-bye to the Palace of San Martin and the man who owns it!"

She could hardly bear to think of Ramón de Lopez, and yet she had not ceased to feel the pressure of his lips on hers.

They had been passionate and demanding, and she wondered if he had felt anything like the same wild rapture that his kiss had caused in her.

Then she told herself that such an idea was ridiculous.

He had kissed many women—alluring, beautiful, seductive women, and as far as she was concerned his kiss had simply been one of gratitude.

It had been automatic; the response expected of a man who had been rescued from imprisonment and possibly death.

He had realised, as she had, that it would have been dangerous to speak, and he had therefore thanked her with his lips and already, Cañuela was sure, he would have forgotten it.

Yet she knew it was something that she would never forget; it would be there in her memory forever.

She tried not to think about the future but she knew that never again would she feel that strange, unaccountable ecstasy; that moment of wonder when she had been part of the sky and the stars.

It was a shock to realise that she had arrived at the Quay, but she saw with satisfaction that a number of ships were making preparations to sail.

With some difficulty a sleepy clerk was found at the Booking-Office.

"Yes, Señorita, the *Hibiscus* will be sailing at seven o'clock. You can board her in half an hour."

"Thank you, Señor."

She produced her ticket and the arrangements were made.

The porter who had taken her luggage from the hackney carriage trundled it in a truck down the Quay to the gang-way of the *Hibiscus*.

Here, however, she found that there was some delay.

No-one was to be allowed aboard until seven o'clock.

She looked at her watch and smiled at the porter.

"I shall just have to wait," she said.

She sat down on the edge of the truck, watching the Quay becoming busier every moment as time passed.

At half past six the porter had a long altercation with a seaman aboard the *Hibiscus*. Then he came back to where Cañuela was still sitting on the truck.

"There will be some further delay, Señorita."

"Oh no!" Cañuela exclaimed in consternation.

"I'm afraid so. Engineering trouble is what they call it. It means she won't sail on time."

Cañuela gave a little sigh of exasperation.

It was what might have been expected, she thought. At the same time she was desperate to get away and to be clear of Buenos Aires before Ramón de Lopez came down for breakfast.

She looked at her watch again. She had been looking at it every ten minutes for the last hour.

"It's no use, Señorita," the porter said. "You won't make time pass any quicker!"

Cañuela laughed and somehow it relieved her tension.

"I must try to wait in patience," she said.

Then as she spoke she thought of Maria.

It seemed impossible that she could have been in Buenos Aires and not visited Maria.

"Will you be kind enough to take care of my luggage?" she said to the porter. "I wish to see a friend who lives not far from here. It should not take me more than half an hour."

"That's all right, Señorita."

Cañuela knew that it would not worry the man to sit by her trunks doing nothing.

In fact it was the sort of job he enjoyed.

He hailed a hackney carriage for her which had just

arrived at the Quay and told the coachman the name of the road.

She was not certain where it was, but the porter knew and directed the driver of the carriage. With a sudden burst of gallantry he also helped Cañuela into it.

"What is the number, Señorita?" he asked.

"Number eighteen," she replied.

Because he had been so helpful she waved her hand to him as she drove away.

Maria's house was in a small, rather squalid street no more than ten minutes from the Quay.

Cañuela had been half-afraid that it would be too early for her to be up, but when she knocked at the door it was opened by her old Nurse.

She was neatly dressed, her grey hair drawn back from her forehead, and she was wearing one of the little linen caps that Cañuela remembered so vividly.

Cañuela pulled off her spectacles.

For a moment Maria looked at her incredulously.

Then she gave a great cry.

"Miss Cañuela! *Mia bambina!* Is it really you? It cannot be true!"

Cañuela put her arms round the little woman and kissed her.

"It is me, Maria! I thought you would be surprised!"

"I am surprised . . . I am delighted . . . it is a happy day for me! Oh, *mia bambina,* I have thought of you so often! How are you . . . and your dear mother?"

Cañuela was drawn into a small room and set down at the table.

Maria bustled about, preparing coffee, talking all the time, the tears running down her cheeks.

"I thought I would never see you again. When you went away so sad, your poor mother in tears, and your father . . ."

Maria dabbed her eyes.

"I think of him and those wicked things that were said about him every day, and I pray for him on my knees every night."

"You know that he is dead?" Cañuela asked.

"I read about it in the newspapers," Maria answered. "May the Mother of Jesus take care of his soul. He was a fine gentleman. I shall never forget him!"

"I shall never forget him either and I thought I would never come back to Buenos Aires."

"But you are here now," Maria said.

"I am just leaving," Cañuela replied. "I have been here for only a few days and now I must return to England and Mama."

She felt that she could not explain to Maria why she had come. It was all too complicated.

Maria was only concerned with the fact that she was going away.

"You are leaving!" she cried. "Oh, my little one, it is good that my eyes have seen you, if only for a minute. You are just as beautiful, but then you always did look like an Angel from Heaven!"

"That is what you used to call me when I was small," Cañuela said. "But now I am older, Maria, it is very difficult to be like an Angel."

"I understand," Maria answered, "you hate the men who were cruel to your dear father. I hate them too. Even though I confess my hatred to the Priest I still go on hating!"

Because Cañuela herself felt like tears she tried to talk of other things.

She told Maria that her mother was not well. How she was in Switzerland and how there was every hope that she would be cured.

Cañuela finished her coffee.

"I must go now, Maria," she said. "It has been lovely to see you. I will write and tell Mama exactly how you are and how you look."

"Tell your Mama," Maria answered, "I think of her all the time and pray for her night and morning."

She gave a sigh.

"I am old, *mia bambina*. There is nothing left for me but memories. Memories of you, your mother, and your father."

Her voice softened when she spoke of Lionel Arlington and Cañuela knew how much the little old Italian woman had adored him.

"He was the most wonderful man in the whole world to me," Maria said. "Look, I keep everything he give me."

She opened a door in a chest which stood in one corner of the tiny room.

She picked up a packet and Cañuela saw that it contained the Christmas-cards they had given her year after year.

There were post-cards they had sent her when they were on holiday and there were drawings that Cañuela had made at some time or another; little sketches that she had done to amuse her father and mother.

Maria had treasured them all.

Then Maria said, a little throb in her voice:

"And this is the last present your dear father ever gave me."

She pulled a package from the back of the drawer, opened it, and Cañuela saw that it was a small china figure.

She remembered all too well how Maria had come by it.

It had been one of a pair, and when dusting in Lionel Arlington's study she had dropped one into the fireplace and burst into tears at her own carelessness.

"*Signor* . . . *Signor* . . . forgive me!" she had cried.

"Do not worry, Maria," Lionel Arlington replied. "To tell the truth I did not care for those china figures."

"I will buy you another, *Signor*. I will save out of my wages."

"You will do nothing of the sort," he answered. "Instead you will oblige me by taking away the figure that is left. In that way neither of us will remember the accident."

Maria had been persuaded to do what he wanted with some reluctance while she still wept over her carelessness.

"I keep it always in the drawer," she told Cañuela. "If I put it on the mantelpiece I might drop it. It is a very treasured memory of your dear father."

"He would be glad that it still gives you pleasure," Cañuela said gently.

Maria started to wrap up the figure again.

Suddenly Cañuela gave a little exclamation.

She put out her hand.

"What is that paper, Maria?" she asked. "Where did you find it?"

Even to herself her voice sounded strange.

Maria looked down at the paper in which the figure had been wrapped.

"It was on the floor in the Sitting-Room," she answered. "When your dear father gave me the figure I looked for something in which to wrap it and found this piece of paper near the waste-paper basket—not in it but lying beside it. I thought it was to be destroyed. Did I do wrong?"

Cañuela drew in her breath.

"No, Maria," she said, "but I would like to have it."

"But of course, *mia bambina*. It is yours!" Maria answered. "You are quite sure it was not wrong for me to have taken it? It was on the floor."

'Yes!' Cañuela thought to herself, 'it was on the floor because it must have been blown there. Blown off Papa's desk to lie beside the waste-paper basket and in consequence cause one of the greatest scandals in the Diplomatic history of the Legation in Buenos Aires!'

It was the map of the harbour with its defensive positions in which Maria had wrapped the china figure. The map which Lionel Arlington had been accused of giving to the Americans!

The map which with the accusations of his colleagues had ruined his career and caused his death.

She took it from Maria's hand and smoothed it out.

For a moment she felt almost faint with the realisation of what this would mean.

Then she rose to her feet.

"I must leave you now, Maria."

"You are going to the ship, Miss Cañuela?"

"No," Cañuela answered. "I am going to the British Legation."

She put her arms round Maria and said:

"Thank you, Maria. Thank you. You have given me something I wanted very much."

Maria did not understand but she wept as Cañuela

drove off in the hackney carriage that had waited for her.

She directed the coachman to the British Legation.

On the way they passed a piece of waste-land and she threw her dark spectacles onto it.

It was a symbolic gesture!

As she stepped down outside the familiar door of the Legation she felt that she had grown inches taller and her chin was high and proud.

"I wish to see the British Minister immediately," she said to the servant.

"I'm afraid that is impossible, Señorita, unless you have an appointment."

"He will see me," Cañuela said. "Will you kindly tell me his name?"

"His Excellency's name," the servant replied, "is Sir Edward Morton, but he will not see you, Señorita."

"Sir Edward!" Cañuela repeated almost beneath her breath, and then she said firmly:

"Kindly inform Sir Edward Morton that Miss Cañuela Arlington is here."

She spoke with such authority that the man, after showing her into a Waiting-Room, obeyed her command.

Cañuela, her eyes alight, waited.

Sir Edward Morton was one of her father's oldest friends. He had been in Buenos Aires when Cañuela was a child, at the Embassy in Madrid when they were there, and again when they returned to Argentina.

He was older than Lionel Arlington but the two men had many interests in common.

Cañuela as a small child had called him "Uncle Edward" because he had become so much a part of the family.

She was not surprised when a few minutes later the servant returned to say that Sir Edward would see her at once.

He led her through the long passages of the Legation to the Minister's private rooms at the back of the house which looked onto a court-yard.

The servant opened a door and Cañuela saw Sir

Edward, a good-looking man with grey hair, standing at the window.

She gave a little cry and ran across the room towards him.

"Cañuela!" he exclaimed. "What are you doing here? I thought there must be some mistake when the servant gave me your name."

"Oh, Uncle Edward! If you only knew how wonderful it is to see you . . . and look what I have brought you."

She held out the map as she spoke. Sir Edward took it from her and stared at it in astonishment.

"Where did you find this? How did you come into possession of it?"

"Maria had it! Oh, Uncle Edward, it hardly seems possible, but Maria had it! You remember Maria?"

"Of course I remember Maria."

"She used it to wrap up a china figure that Papa gave her. She found it lying on the floor beside the waste-paper basket and thought it was a piece of paper to be thrown away. It was with her all the time!"

"It sounds incredible!" Sir Edward said. "But where have you been—you and your mother? I have been looking for you—searching for you. You vanished!"

"We were so humiliated and so upset by Papa's death."

"I can understand that," Sir Edward said. "My dear, the Foreign Office wants to make reparation."

Cañuela was suddenly still.

"Reparation?"

He nodded his head.

"Janson Mandell had a carriage accident last year. Before he died he confessed."

Cañuela drew in her breath.

"He confessed that he invented the story of your father's treachery," Sir Edward went on, "because he felt your father had insulted him."

"I felt it must be something like that," Cañuela said almost in a whisper.

Sir Edward looked down at the map.

"The only thing missing was the map," he said, "and now the Foreign Office will make full reparation for any stigma on your father's name, and of course there will be a pension for your mother."

There were tears in Cañuela's eyes, then she said in a voice which broke:

"That will not bring back . . . Papa."

"I know that," Sir Edward said, "but it should make it easier for both of you. Where is your mother?"

"She is in Switzerland," Cañuela replied. "She has been ill, Uncle Edward, but if anything will make her recover quickly it will be this news. She minded so desperately about Papa."

"In Switzerland!" Sir Edward repeated. "As it happens, Cañuela, I am going to Geneva next week. I can see your mother. I can explain to her what has happened."

"That would be wonderful!" Cañuela cried. "You know how fond Mama has always been of you."

"And I of her," Sir Edward answered. "I have always loved your mother more than anyone else in the world."

"Is that why you never married, Uncle Edward?"

He nodded his head and suddenly Cañuela bent forward to kiss his cheek.

"Dear Uncle Edward . . . perhaps after all this time you and Mama can find a little happiness together. She has been so lonely . . . so terribly lonely since Papa died."

Sir Edward's arm tightened round her shoulders.

He did not speak and Cañuela knew that it was difficult for him to find words.

There was the sound of voices arguing in the corridor outside and then the door burst open.

Ramón de Lopez stood there and Cañuela knew that the servants had tried to prevent him from entering.

He stood looking at her and there was an expression on his face which she did not understand.

"De Lopez!" Sir Edward exclaimed. "You could not have come at a better moment. There is news—very good news indeed. I know how delighted you will be."

Ramón de Lopez did not reply and Sir Edward went on:

"You fought so hard to prove Lionel Arlington's

innocence, and now the last link in the chain has been discovered. The map!"

He held it up as he spoke and added triumphantly: "The map we all searched for so arduously!"

"Where was it?"

It seemed as if the words were dragged from Ramón de Lopez's lips. His eyes were still on Cañuela.

"Cañuela found it . . ." Sir Edward began, and then said:

"I forgot—you do not know each other. Cañuela, this is Ramón de Lopez—a very dear friend of your father's—who always believed that he had been slandered and unjustly persecuted. Ramón, this is Cañuela Arlington—Lionel Arlington's daughter!"

"We have met!" Ramón de Lopez said.

"What I am going to do," Sir Edward said to Cañuela, "is to send a cable immediately to the Foreign Office telling them the map has been restored to us, and now there is nothing to prevent them from making a public announcement exonerating your father from all the lies that have been circulating about him. I know they will do that, because I spoke to the Foreign Secretary last time I was in England."

"I also spoke to him," Ramón de Lopez said, coming further in to the room, "and when I was in England I engaged a private detective to try to discover the whereabouts of Mrs. Arlington and her daughter, Cañuela."

"Why should you have done that?" Cañuela asked.

"Because I believed in your father," he answered.

"But you never answered his letter," she said. "He wrote to you asking your help and you never replied."

"I was in Uruguay. I had to go there unexpectedly, and when I returned I found your father's letter, but the ship which carried you home had already left."

Cañuela gave a little sigh.

It seemed such a reasonable explanation and yet neither she nor her mother had ever thought of it.

They had just accepted that Ramón de Lopez had turned against her father as all his other so-called friends had done.

"And now, Cañuela," Sir Edward said, "you must

explain to me what you are doing in Buenos Aires and where you are staying."

"She is staying with me," Ramón de Lopez said.

There was something in his voice that was decisive and authoritative.

There was to be no argument about it!

She would stay with him!

EIGHT

Outside the British Legation, Cañuela saw an open Cabriolet drawn by four horses.

It was a vehicle of the latest fashion she had not seen before in Buenos Aires but she knew was much favoured in London as a smart and rapid mode of travel.

The body of the carriage was very light, the wheels were large, and she knew that it would move with great speed and at the same time great comfort over rough roads.

She was however surprised to see that Ramón de Lopez was driving four horses in the centre of Buenos Aires.

He helped her into the Cabriolet and the groom who was holding the horses then jumped up behind them.

This meant, Cañuela knew, that anything they said to each other could be overheard and in a way she was glad that the servant was there.

There were, she knew, many explanations she had to make and many questions that Ramón de Lopez would ask of her.

But at the moment she was so elated and so thrilled that her father's name had been cleared that it was a relief that was beyond words.

In fact it was impossible to think of anything except that the cloud that had encompassed her and her mother for so long had lifted.

Now there was no need for subterfuge, no need for disguise, and she could be herself and proud of it!

Ramón de Lopez drove his horses comparatively

slowly through the heavy traffic, but with an expertise that was undeniable.

Then to Cañuela's surprise they did not turn into the Plaza St. Martin but drove away down one of the long straight streets which she knew would take them out of the city.

She looked at him enquiringly, but at the same time she felt a little afraid of what seemed to be a rather serious expression on his face.

Perhaps he was angry with her, she thought, and then asked herself why it should matter.

Now that he knew who she was, they could meet on equal terms and she need no longer be subservient to his moods or indeed his irritation with her.

Then she knew that if she had been vulnerable before she was still more vulnerable now.

She loved him, and while in the past she could tell herself that he was only buying her services, now she was bound to him by a far deeper bond.

That of the love which made her feel weak and helpless simply because she was sitting beside him.

They reached the outskirts of the city and at last her curiosity could be restrained no longer.

"Where are we going?" she asked.

"To the *Estancia*," he replied.

As he spoke four horsemen appeared.

Cañuela looked at them in sudden fear before she realised that they were wearing the clothes in which Ramón de Lopez dressed his *gauchos*.

There was a great deal of silver on their saddles, their harnesses, and their coats. She saw too that every man carried in his belt a pistol and a knife.

As if he understood what she was thinking Ramón de Lopez said:

"I am taking no risks, and we are, as you can see, well protected from attack."

"I am glad," Cañuela murmured beneath her breath.

"Not that the particular gentlemen who kidnapped me will trouble us for some time," Ramón de Lopez went on. "They were captured last night by the Military and those who were not wanted for more grievous crimes will undoubtedly spend a great number of years in prison."

"What sort of crimes?" Cañuela asked.

"Three of them were murderers!" he answered casually.

She felt her heart almost stop at the thought that they might have murdered him.

Again as if he realised what she was thinking he smiled at her in a manner that she found irresistible as he said:

"It is entirely due to you that I am here, so I will take no chances either with myself—or you."

There was something in the way in which he spoke the last word that made Cañuela look away from him shyly, her eyes on the horses.

Then he added with a hint of laughter in his voice:

"In case you are worrying about your trunks, they have already gone ahead!"

"You found them?" he asked.

"I arrived at the Quay to learn from the porter where you had gone. My groom collected the luggage and on my instructions it has been sent on to the *Estancia* to await your arrival."

Cañuela wanted to say how much she was looking forward to seeing the *Estancia,* but for some reason she could not explain to herself she found it hard to speak.

"Your Italian Nurse told me you were at the British Legation," Ramón de Lopez went on. "She also told me who you were."

Again Cañuela found that she had nothing to say.

She was conscious that the groom could hear their every word, and all the questions that rushed into her mind seemed too intimate to be overheard by a servant.

As if he understood, Ramón de Lopez said no more but concentrated on driving his horses at a tremendous pace, while their escorts galloped beside them.

They left behind them a cloud of dust which seemed to hover over the softly moving grasses of the Pampas.

They reached the *Estancia* in what Cañuela was sure was record time.

At first it was only a purple shadow on the horizon

which seemed to shimmer in the sunshine as if it were an island surrounded by the sea.

Then there was the first sight of the high, centuries-old Lombardy poplars, which were conspicuous at a great distance.

As they drew nearer Cañuela could see acacia, peach, quince, and cherry trees.

Some were in blossom and exceedingly beautiful, and she realised that the trees which enclosed the *Estancia* must stretch for perhaps half a mile on either side of it.

There was a long, cool avenue twisting up to the house and when she saw it she remembered that her father had told her it was one of the most beautiful *Estancias* in the whole of Argentina.

In the gardens surrounding the house, the flowers, brilliant in the sunshine, were breathtakingly beautiful.

The *Estancia* itself had two towers on either side of it, which gave it an almost Medieval appearance.

The front of the building with its carved pillars and arched openings was as beautiful as she might have expected.

Ramón de Lopez drew up his horses with a flourish outside the front door, and a crowd of servants streamed out to welcome them, to run to the horses' heads, or usher them into the cool, dim Hall which was redolent with the fragrance of flowers.

Beyond the Hall Cañuela could see a court-yard with a fountain which even at a glance seemed to her more beautiful than the one in the Plaza St. Martin.

She turned to Ramón de Lopez to try to discover what was expected of her.

Unexpectedly he reached out to take her hand in his.

"You had very little sleep last night," he said in a gentle voice which was also caressing. "I suggest that you go to your room and rest. Our marriage will take place in the evening at seven o'clock!"

The words were such a shock that Cañuela could only stare at him, her eyes very wide in her pale face.

He raised her hand and she felt his lips against her skin.

Instinctively her fingers tightened on his like those of a child who is afraid of what lies ahead.

Then a voice she recognised said beside her:

"If you will come with me, Señorita, I will show you your bed-room."

It was Dolores who stood there, and it seemed to Cañuela that the maid swept her away. Though there were many things she wished to say and hear from Ramón de Lopez, it was impossible to do anything but follow her.

The court-yard through which they passed was lovelier than she could have imagined any *Estancia*, however old, could be.

There was not only a carved fountain but statues, urns, and exquisitely tiled paving, all of white marble, glowing against the brilliance of the flowers.

She was however too bemused to take in anything; too shocked by Ramón de Lopez's words even to be able to think.

The bed-room into which Dolores led her was very large, white, and cool, the blinds drawn against the heat of the sun.

It was still comparatively early in the morning, but later in the day the sun could, as Cañuela well knew, be intense.

"I have not yet finished unpacking, Señorita," Dolores said, "but as the Señor says that you are to sleep, I shall finish what has to be done in another room."

"I am . . . surprised to see you . . . here, Dolores."

"The Señor knew that I would see to your clothes better than a stranger," Dolores explained.

She started to help Cañuela out of her travelling-gown and as she did so there came a knock at the door.

There was a servant outside with food on a tray and some wine.

Cañuela was about to say that she needed nothing, and then she realised that she was in fact quite hungry.

She had eaten no breakfast and very little the night before.

Besides, Dolores was determined that she should

carry out the Señor's instructions and Cañuela still felt too confused to argue.

It was not until Dolores had left her and she was finally alone in the cool dimness of the bed-room that she began to think coherently.

Ramón de Lopez had said that their marriage would take place this evening!

How could he have arranged it without consulting her or even asking her to be his wife?

Then as she thought of him she knew there was nothing she wanted more than to be in his arms; to feel his lips on hers as they had been last night when he had kissed her as they escaped from the tunnel.

"I love him! I love him!" she told herself. "But how do I know that he loves me?"

Could he really have felt the same magic that she had felt when their lips met?

For one brief moment the whole world had stopped still and there was no danger, no fear, no difficulties, only an ecstasy which had been beyond expression.

She thought of the firmness that had been in his voice when he had said to Sir Edward:

"She is staying with me!"

And she remembered too the expression on his face when he had walked into the room at the Legation.

Trying to explain it to herself, she had thought that there had been relief that he had found her there, together with a look of determination that he should get his own way, which she knew so well would mean that he was at his most obstinate, and there was something else. . . .

Could it be love?

She could hardly believe it; hardly credit that he should love her; for except for one kiss no expression of love had ever passed between them.

Yet she felt her whole body yearning for him, and thinking of him she fell asleep. . . .

It seemed to Cañuela that she had slept for only a short time when Dolores woke her, but it had in fact been nearly eight hours!

She had gone to sleep worrying, but she woke with a feeling of irrepressible gaiety rising within her.

"Everything is ready, Señorita," Dolores said.

Cañuela looked at her as if waiting for an explanation and she went on:

"You will of course be married in that lovely white gown which was in your luggage."

"My mother's gown," Cañuela said half to herself.

She thought it was indeed fitting that it should be her wedding-dress.

The gown which her mother had never worn, but which she had thought Cañuela would wear to a Ball.

Perhaps, Cañuela thought to herself, with some uncanny foresight, her mother had known that it was essential that she should take it with her.

Dolores had prepared her bath. It was scented with jasmine, which the maid told her grew profusely in the court-yards of the *Estancia*.

Dolores arranged her hair high on her head as the Spaniards wore it on festive occasions.

Cañuela understood why when, having put on her mother's white gown with its soft tulle framing her bare shoulders, Dolores produced a wedding-veil.

It was Spanish in design, short and full to fall from a high comb.

Instead of the comb there was a tiara of diamonds which Cañuela learnt was a present from Ramón de Lopez.

"It is a family jewel, Señorita," Dolores explained, "and belonged to the Señor's great-great-great grandmother when she came with the Señor's ancestor from Spain to conquer Argentina."

It was fashioned in a design of flowers, but at the same time the tiara looked very regal.

When Cañuela rose from the dressing-table she walked across the room to where there was a long mirror.

She stared at herself and realised that nothing could be more becoming than the white satin gown with its tiny waist, exquisitely draped skirt, and the Spanish veil falling over her shoulders.

The fiery lights in her hair seemed to echo the

sparkle of the diamonds and the brilliance of her eyes.

At the same time her expression, a little shy, a little apprehensive, was that of a very young girl stepping into the unknown, uncertain as to what the future would hold.

"You are ready, Señorita?" Dolores asked softly.

"What do I do . . . now?" Cañuela asked, suddenly afraid.

"The Señor is waiting for you downstairs. It is unusual, but he himself is taking you to the Church."

Dolores opened the bed-room door.

Outside on the balcony a small boy dressed in the swaggering costume of a *gaucho* stood holding a bouquet in his hand.

It was of small white lilies, and Cañuela wondered if Ramón de Lopez had remembered when he ordered them that he had told her she looked like *Lágrimas de la Virgen.*

It would have been impossible for her to have carried those because their petals dropped at the touch of a human hand.

The small lilies were, however, not unlike them and she felt as if somehow they conveyed a message to her.

Very slowly she walked along the balcony and down the stairs. Then as she reached the court-yard Ramón de Lopez was waiting for her.

He came to her framed against the rising waters of the fountain, iridescent in the gleaming red of the setting sun.

For a moment he seemed so big and overwhelming that she was afraid.

Then she realised that it was because for the first time she was seeing him in the clothes of a *gaucho,* and that nothing could have become him better.

The short black jacket, full breeches over leather boots, and wide red sash with silver ornamentations made him look even more romantic, exciting, and masculine than he had done before.

He was standing very still and Cañuela found that she could no longer move.

Their eyes met and it seemed that there was no need for words; no need for explanations.

"You are more beautiful than I can ever begin to tell you!" he said very quietly.

She felt her heart turn over in her breast. Then he offered her his arm and she put her fingers on it.

They went through the Hall to where outside there was waiting an open carriage which was decorated with flowers.

The two horses which drew it were garlanded and the coachman who was driving them wore a flower in his top-hat.

Ramón de Lopez helped Cañuela into the carriage and they set off, driving down the long avenue of flowering trees to where in the distance she could see the towers of an ancient Church.

Ramón de Lopez did not take her hand nor did he speak.

She had the feeling that he was preparing himself for the ceremony that lay ahead, and that there was something spiritual in his silence.

It took only a few moments to reach the Church. Outside it there was a crowd all dressed in their best for the occasion.

The red skirts and embroidered blouses of the women, bright against the black of the *gauchos'* jackets, were complemented by the gay colours of the men who laboured in the gardens and fruit groves of the *Estancia.*

The Church was full.

It was not a large one and it seemed to Cañuela as Ramón de Lopez led her up the aisle that a sea of faces turned almost like the movements of waves as the music started.

Because she was shy she bent her head a little and her fingers tightened on his arm.

As if he understood he covered her hand with his, and she felt as if he gave her both comfort and strength.

The Altar was ablaze with candles and Cañuela saw that the whole of the Chancel was decorated with lilies.

The fragrance of them was almost overpowering and she was sure that Ramón de Lopez had chosen them especially for her.

The marriage-ceremony was not long because he was a Catholic and she was not, but as they took their marriage-vows Cañuela prayed that they would be blessed.

She had always had the feeling that Ramón de Lopez was seeking something; asking for something which was out of his reach.

Now she prayed that it might be herself.

'Help me, God, to make him happy,' she whispered in her heart.

She thought as he said the words "and with my body I thee worship" there was a depth of sincerity in his voice which she had never heard before.

They moved back down the aisle to the music of the organ, and as they reached the outside of the Church the noise and excitement of the Argentines was almost deafening.

People cheered and shouted, clapped and cried out in their enthusiasm.

As they drove away together towards the *Estancia* the whole population followed them.

It was impossible to speak above the noise or to do anything but smile and wave to their well-wishers.

They also had to protect themselves from the showers of flower petals which were thrown until the whole carriage was filled with them.

They entered the *Estancia* by a different door and now Cañuela found herself in a huge court-yard which was decorated with flags and bunting, flowers and lanterns.

Already the sun had set and the dusk was giving way to night.

The lanterns cast a golden glow and Cañuela saw that a huge feast had been prepared round the main court-yard.

Ramón de Lopez took her to a table where there were two seats like thrones. What seemed like hundreds of guests seated themselves and the feast began.

There was a whole ox being roasted over a fire in one corner of the court-yard. There were the traditional dishes of Argentina, some of which Cañuela remembered, some of which she had never tasted before.

There was fish prepared in the Spanish way, corvina and pescadilla, which were everybody's favourites, and large quantities of mussels, bivalve molluscs, snails, cholgas, and cuttle-fish.

Fresh red shrimps, craw fish, and crabs were sought at festival-time not only as food but as a decoration.

Naturally to end the meal there was the *"Dulce de Leche,"* the famous Argentine jam made with milk and sugar which was a favourite not only with every child in the country but also with their parents.

There were barrels of wine and everyone seemed to be laughing.

Cañuela had never known Ramón de Lopez to be so gay.

One after another the men came to drink to his health and he had a joke and something personal to say to each one of them.

She realised, watching him, that here was the secret of a successful *Estancia,* where the owner was not the master but on equal terms with his men and there was a cameraderie that was not translatable into words.

While they ate there was the soft music of guitars and violins.

As the last plates were removed from the tables the music became louder and Cañuela realised that everyone round the room was looking at them expectantly.

She turned towards Ramón de Lopez for explanation and he smiled at her.

"They are waiting for us to start the dancing," he said.

He rose as he spoke and led her into the centre of the court-yard.

The floor was of polished marble and she knew that it would be easy to dance on it.

He put his arms round her and the Band played the opening bars of a tango.

"Our second dance together," he said in a deep voice.

She looked up at him in surprise.

"Did you . . . know?"

"Do you imagine I could touch you and not be aware of it?" he asked, and she felt herself quiver at the passion in his voice.

Then they were dancing as they had danced at his Ball, but with a difference.

They were closer. Now it was almost as if he was wooing her without words but with the sensuous movements of the tango.

She felt as if she vibrated not only to the pressure of his hands but to the thoughts of his mind.

She knew that the desire within herself for them to be alone and still closer was also in him.

The very melody of the music was part of their desire, the steps were the enticement, the anticipation, the realisation of love.

They finished the tango alone. Then the applause rang out loud and exhilarating, echoing round the court-yard and up into the darkness of the star-strewn sky.

Then as everybody else surged onto the dance floor Ramón de Lopez drew Cañuela aside.

Almost before she was aware of it they had left the court-yard with its golden lanterns and were moving through the deserted passages of the *Estancia* back through court-yard after court-yard.

They reached the one where the fountain played and where Cañuela knew her bed-room was situated.

Ramón de Lopez did not pause but drew her up the stairs and along the balcony.

He opened the door and she was assailed by the fragrance of lilies.

Since she had left for the Church the room had been decorated.

There were only two candelabra burning on either side of the huge bed with its white draperies and gold corona of Angels, but there were lilies everywhere—around the walls, on the chests, and in great vases on the dressing-table.

She turned to thank Ramón de Lopez, to find that he was standing a little away from her and the expression on his face made the words die on her lips.

"You are so beautiful," he said softly, "that I am afraid."

"Afraid . . . ?"

"That you are like *Lágrimas de la Virgen,* which no man may touch."

She waited, her eyes on his, her breath coming quickly between her parted lips as he walked very slowly across the intervening space between them.

"Shall I find out for certain?" he asked.

She quivered but she could not answer him.

Very gently he took the tiara from her head and drew the veil from her hair.

"You are mine," he said, "as I always meant you to be. How could you think you could escape me?"

He put his arms round her and drew her close.

She thought he was going to kiss her and knew that she wanted his lips more than she had ever wanted anything in her life.

Instead he drew the pins from her hair so that it fell onto her shoulders as it had the night he had come into her cabin.

His hands were very gentle.

Then just as gently he put his fingers under her chin and lifted up her face to his.

"I love you!" he said, and his lips were on hers.

For a moment they were tender, and then, as Cañuela felt the magic and the wonder that she had known the night before rise within her, his mouth became more demanding, more possessive.

A flame so ecstatic, so rapturous, burnt its way through her body until she felt once again as if the world whirled round them and vanished.

She was no longer conscious of the room, or the lilies, she knew only that she was his.

She belonged to him and her love was wild as the wind blowing over the Pampas, violent as the waves of the sea, and deep as the darkness of the night.

"I love you! Dear God, how I love you!"

His voice made her tremble with the ecstasy of desire.

His mouth possessed her again and now she felt him undoing her gown.

He held her closer still and the white dress which had belonged to her mother slipped like a shaft of moonlight to the ground.

He kissed her neck, her shoulders, her breasts.

Lifting her in his arms, he carried her against his heart to the white bed.

The soft note of an owl hooting in the distance made Cañuela stir against Ramón de Lopez's bare shoulder.

It was the grey-and-white owl whose hoot sounded like the coo of a wood-pigeon.

"Do you remember . . ." she whispered.

"I told you that you looked like a little wise owl!" he answered. "I used to lie awake at night wondering what your eyes were like. I could not believe they were as beautiful as your mouth."

She felt herself thrill.

"When did you first . . . love me?"

His arms tightened about her.

"I know now that I fell in love with your voice when you spoke to me in Spanish," he answered. "It was musical, lovely, and somehow alluring as a woman's voice had never been alluring to me before."

He smiled and added:

"Afterwards it became cold and distant and was meant to be repressive."

"You said I was . . . like a . . . *frigorifico*."

"That was how your voice sounded. At the same time your lips curved sweetly and told me you could never really be cold. I was right!"

Cañuela blushed and turned her face against him.

"You . . . made me . . . so . . . excited!"

"Do I really excite you—wildly, passionately, as you excite me?"

"You . . . know . . . you do."

"I will teach you to love me, my beloved sweetheart, until the fire in your eyes is as bright as the fire in your hair."

"I would . . . like . . . that."

"If you only knew how afraid I was that you really disliked me!"

"I told myself I . . . hated you because you had . . . betrayed Papa."

"How could you imagine such a thing?" Ramón de

Lopez asked. "I had a deep affection for your father. I fought in every possible way to prove that the slanders that were uttered about him were untrue."

His arms tightened again.

"How could you and your mother have hidden yourselves away so completely? Everyone in the Foreign Office both here and in England were looking for you and so was I."

"We could not face a world that would . . . believe such . . . things about Papa."

"Now the world will acknowledge your father and admire him."

Cañuela gave a deep sigh.

"I can hardly believe that all the . . . misery and unhappiness is . . . over."

"You will never be unhappy again," Ramón de Lopez vowed.

"Never?"

"I shall love you, adore you, and worship you for as long as we live—will that make you happy?"

"You know it . . . will!"

"I love every tiny scrap of you—your fascinating, stimulating brain, your exquisite body, and your adorable, lovely face!"

"Is it . . . true what you are . . . saying to me?"

Cañuela's voice was that of a child waiting to be reassured.

"It is true, my precious."

"You never . . . asked me to . . . marry you. How did you know I . . . loved you?"

"I asked you without words," he answered. "When you helped me to escape—and I could not believe that a woman could be so brave or so clever—I kissed you."

Cañuela drew in her breath at the memory.

"When your lips touched mine," he went on, "they told me, my darling, that you loved me. That was all I needed to know."

"But I could . . . never have . . . married you unless Papa's . . . name had been cleared!"

"You would have married me."

"You could not marry . . . someone who was under

a . . . cloud, whom people . . . believed to be the daughter of a . . . traitor."

"Do you think it would matter to me if you were the daughter of the devil himself or of a beggar in the Boca?"

"I would not have . . . married you."

"Then I would have kidnapped you. I intended you to be my wife and I would never have let you go."

She thrilled at the possessive masterfulness in his voice.

"Now you are my wife!" he went on. "I have never, and this is the truth, my precious darling, asked a woman to marry me, or even wanted to marry one, until I met you. I already loved you before I saw you that night when I came to your cabin."

"How . . . could you have?" Cañuela asked.

"One does not love only with one's eyes," Ramón de Lopez answered. "A man loves instinctively with his heart and with his soul."

His fingers stroked her hair as he said:

"When I saw you with that baby in your arms it was like a blinding light. I knew I had found what I had always been seeking. I knew that you were the woman who belonged to me; the perfect manifestation of the ideal which stood in a secret shrine of my heart where no-one else had ever entered."

There was a depth in his voice that seemed to vibrate between them.

Again Cañuela hid her face against his shoulder.

After a moment he said in a very different tone:

"You are crying! My darling—what have I said? What have I done to hurt you?"

"It is . . . because I am so . . . happy," Cañuela sobbed. "Because you say such . . . wonderful . . . things to me. I thought I could never . . . be married and now I am your . . . wife."

Her voice broke and Ramón de Lopez held her even closer, his lips against her hair.

"You have been through so much," he said tenderly, "and the strain of hiding yourself all this time must have been intolerable. It is all over now, my beautiful, adorable little wife."

"I am so . . . happy . . . so marvellously, gloriously . . . happy," Cañuela said, but her voice still broke a little on the words.

Then she said almost accusingly:

"You . . . wanted me to cry."

"Those are the tears of love."

Cañuela raised her head.

"You knew that was what . . . *Lágrimas de la Virgen* are sometimes . . . called?"

"Of course I knew it," he answered. "And could anything be more perfect, more wonderful, than that you should shed them for me?"

"I love . . . you!" Cañuela whispered.

"And I love you!" he answered. "There are so many things for us to do together, my darling—together in every way."

"When we danced together I felt that I was a . . . part of you."

"As you are, and as you always will be. And now I am no longer afraid."

She smiled.

"You know that I can be . . . touched by human hands?"

"You can be touched only by my hands," he corrected, "and I would kill anyone else who attempted it."

"All I want is to be . . . with you . . . to belong to . . . you."

"You are mine—mine until the stars fall from the sky and there is no longer any grass on the Pampas. Mine, my darling! Now and for all eternity."

His lips were on hers, his hands were touching her, his heart was beating against hers.

There was nothing left but the ecstasy of belonging, the wild, passionate rapture of being one.

ABOUT THE AUTHOR

BARBARA CARTLAND, the celebrated romantic author, historian, playwright, lecturer, political speaker and television personality, has now written over 150 books. Miss Cartland has had a number of historical books published and several biographical ones, including that of her brother, Major Ronald Cartland, who was the first Member of Parliament to be killed in the War. This book had a Foreword by Sir Winston Churchill.

In private life, Barbara Cartland, who is a Dame of the Order of St. John of Jerusalem, has fought for better conditions and salaries for Midwives and Nurses. As President of the Royal College of Midwives (Hertfordshire Branch), she has been invested with the first Badge of Office ever given in Great Britain, which was subscribed to by the Midwives themselves. She has also championed the cause for old people and founded the first Romany Gypsy Camp in the world.

Barbara Cartland is deeply interested in Vitamin Therapy and is President of the British National Association for Health.